Women of the Revolution

The Scottish Agent

Book 2: 1790

A Novel by Julie MP Adams

Copyright 2023 Julie MP Adams

The moral right of JMP Adams to be identified as the author of this work has been asserted in accordance with the Copyright, Designs and Patents Act, 1988.

All rights reserved. No part of this publication may be reproduced or transmitted in any form or by any means, electronic or mechanical without permission in writing from the publisher.

This book is a work of fiction. Names, characters, businesses, organizations, places and events are either the product of the author's imagination or used fictitiously. Any resemblance to actual persons, living or dead, events or locales is entirely coincidental.

Books by Julie Adams

The Lapidary
Malbister
Into The Woods
Broken Wings
The Scottish Agent Book 1: 1789

Characters

Andrew Cargill, a sea captain
Jessamine Cargill, his wife, an heiress to mills in Scotland
Jacob Rose, Usher to the French Assembly
Jean the clerk, Jacob's assistant.
Jacques Rose—Jean's twin—an agent provocateur.
Sandy Geddes, a Scottish merchant in Paris
Francine, his wife
George Rose, assistant to William Pitt the Younger
Suzanne Gregoire
Le Maitre, a printer and agent provocateur
Jeanne de la Motte
Virginie De La Croix Deschamps
George Rose, cousin of Jacob and assistant to William Pitt the Younger
The Mill owner—father of Jessamine Cargill
The button maker—a London artisan
Olympe de Gouges
Joseph Bologna, Chevalier de Saint Georges
Abbe Raynal
Marie Joseph Rose Beauharnais
Manon Roland

To the late Sinclair Swanson, History teacher extraordinaire, with thanks

Prologue

January, 1790
Arbroath

The main gates of Arbroath Abbey tower over visitors and never fail to impress. Even that old curmudgeon Samuel Johnson admitted the ruins were a reminder of past grandeur. Of course, the days of the Abbey's magnificence- when it was in effect the seat of Scottish government- are firmly in the past.

Cargill, twisting his tricorn hat in his hands, reflects on the fate of the Abbot Beaton, who as Cardinal tried to quash the Reformers: Hamilton, Wishart and Knox, but paid for it with his life. Some things you cannot stop, try as you will.

Like most of the Arbroath townsfolk, Cargill was raised in the Church of Scotland. Lately there are more church buildings springing up to accommodate the splinter groups breaking away from the Kirk: Cameronians; Auld Lichts; New Lichts; Free Church and so on. All these new churches confuse him. What's the point of breaking away because someone disapproves of singing or the form of prayer?

He recalls a conversation at Sandy Geddes' table, on a recent voyage when he brought documents to Paris. Their mutual friend Jacob Rose was explaining how the Scottish Enlightenment is entwined with the notions coming from Switzerland. It was Swiss John Calvin and his ideas that emboldened Knox and his like to remove the de Guise queen and Cardinal Beaton. Those ideas gave Scotland a Church where all men were equal and could read, write and interpret Scripture for themselves, instead of through Latin chanting and ritual.

The Swiss Jean Jacques Rousseau's Social Contract is essential reading for the members of the Paris Assembly, as is the work of the Scots Philosophers, Jacob tells them. There can be no liberty, equality and fraternity without those founding principles.

As they sipped their after-dinner cognac, Cargill asked, 'Do you go to Kirk, here in Paris?' For centuries, the French Protestants were suppressed, with many fleeing to Spitalfields in London, or to the Netherlands.

Jacob nodded, 'They've stopped persecuting the Huguenots, but we Scots have our own little Kirk, tending to our needs. We don't call attention to ourselves, but the Reverend Johnson does good work among our little community. Why do you ask?'

Jacob followed Cargill's gaze – towards the panelled double doors, newly opened. The ladies in that room were served cups of chocolate by a page in velvet livery. Sandy's wife Francine's guests tonight included her sister and her friend the Marquise, who takes the little boy Etienne everywhere. He's a head taller than when Cargill took him away from his mother at the harbour in Hispaniola. 'You're wondering what the Kirk thinks about slavery?' Jacob asks.

Women of the Revolution

'And your Assembly. Surely with all these Rights of Man, something must change?'

Cargill turns from the main gate and stumps through the archway with the squat tower on the right, before opening the little iron gate that gives access to the former Abbot's House, that these days is a thread factory. Nothing is wasted in this town- after the reformation the fabric of the Abbey was either used for building or what remained intact sold off. He contemplates the iron studded door for a while before grasping the ring handle and pushing it open.

At first, he's almost deafened by the clacking of the machinery, as he climbs the stairs to the former Abbot's study. The man he's come to see sits at his vast oak desk, quill in hand, poring over a ledger and making entries in a spidery copperplate. He's removed his hat, and his powdered wig is slightly askew. His nose is redder than usual. To his left is a flagon and a tankard. Cargill wonders how much his father-in-law has had to drink?

The older man looks up, takes notice and indicates a chair in the corner of the room. Cargill drags it over to the other side of the desk, and the scraping screech makes them both wince.

'That last cargo of yours was three bales short,' he remarks. No formal greeting for a son in law who has come to report in rather than go straight home.

He responds, 'Aye, well, that was all that was in the warehouse. The flax harvest was poor.'

A grunt, and then the older man tips the rest of the flagon into the tankard and takes a hearty swig. He does not bother to offer any refreshment to Cargill. 'We'll need to buy from elsewhere. This order won't spin itself out of thin air. The cloth is needed in Charleston for the end of May.'

Sixteen weeks away, means less time at home, and sailing in bad weather, something Cargill is used to, but his crew is short of two men, taken by press gangs while ashore to get provisions. They'd gone for a drink, the fools, and now he'll need to seek replacements, preferably men who know the sea.

At least it will be a cargo of cloth- Osnaburg linen, woven in the Arbroath mills. He's done his share of taking those poor souls from West Africa.

'The usual cargo when we offload the cloth?' he asks.

'Aye. Tobacco's fetching a good price. See if you can bring back some molasses, and sugar loaf. Rum, if you can get it in the islands? The Navy office pays well for that.'

A pause. 'There are passages booked both ways. You'll pick up your first passenger at Le Havre on the way there. He'll be going as far as Folkestone with you. There will be another two from Saint Domingue on your way back. It will be in the ship's papers.'

No details of who will be sailing with them. The old man plays his cards close to his chest, but in the past, he's had government spies on board, as well as house slaves taken from the West Indies to France.

'You'll be wanting to spend time with your family before you sail again.' That isn't a question- it's an order. Cargill nods, stands up, and moves toward the door. 'We'll see you at dinner on Sunday.'

Cargill descends the stair, planting his hat on his head once outside the door. There's a keen wind blowing as he walks past the gatehouse to the High Street – a jumble of buildings, some of which were built from the Abbey stones by thrifty masons. He pauses at the door of the inn, but Jessamine will have word by now that her man's home from the sea and will be waiting for him in their new house on Market Gate. She'll know that he went to see her father before going home, and she'll be vexed. He reflects it's better to keep in his wife's good graces.

Women of the Revolution

They've three of a family: two girls, and the one boy, the same age as Etienne. Why can't he get that page out of his mind? Is it the fact that he knows his wee Stephen hasn't had such a hard life? Or is it the memory of a distraught mother, wailing in agony on the quayside while her brave son swore he'd return to look after her?

Is now the time to tell his father-in-law he wants nothing more to do with the slave trade?

The spirit of Revolution in Paris has not gone unnoticed in London. At that dinner, Jacob spoke of his cousin George, who works in the office of William Pitt the Younger. Last year, a mutual friend, William Wilberforce gave a three-hour speech in Parliament condemning slavery and calling for its abolition. Pitt supported him, but his attempts failed. Too many slave owning interests control the Rotten Boroughs. There are seats in Parliament that are in the gift of landowners, who tell the dozen or so voters who to return at elections. It makes a mockery of politics, and until there is Parliamentary Reform, there can be no change.

'Take heart,' Jacob told him. 'Change will come. They can only resist for so long. Look at the men of business and letters. How long will they put up without representation?' He has a point. The big northern cities of Manchester and Liverpool, not to mention Glasgow are thriving manufacturing centres, and for the wealthy men who control industry not to have their voices heard in Parliament is grossly unfair.

Cargill takes pride in the white walls of their new house. It's close to the harbour, but has three storeys and symmetrical windows, all still with glass, unlike a neighbour who bricked several up to avoid the window tax.

Jessamine is at the door and he tries to read her expression. She's approaching forty- when they wed, she was past the first flush of youth. Her light brown hair is turning to ash blonde under the lace edged cap he brought back from France, along with other luxuries like silk for a dress, and the perfumed oils she places in dishes on the mantel.

He goes to embrace her, but she offers her cheek to kiss. She's expecting company, and he's to go and find the lad, who sneaked out with the dog to look for him, when news came the ship was in harbour.

Like father, like daughter. Jess hardly bothers to notice he's there- until she wants something from him.

Chapter 1

February, 1790
London

Misery is the cheapest room of a Clerkenwell lodging house. The two women who sit on chairs by the window are in deshabille, with their stays unlaced and their loose backed dressing robes fastened to protect modesty.

On the spindly legged table between them, a silver teapot and two delicate cups and saucers indicate that they have been taking tea, that most civilised of activities. They've shared a single cake, and there is no milk. There's a fire laid in the grate, but it is unlit, saving precious coals until later.

Until this month, they had a room each, on the floor below. They shared the services of a maid, who helped them dress and knew how to style hair. Now they occupy this one small room in the attics and take turns in helping one other lace stays and tidy locks. The bed is small: a truckle is stowed underneath it.

On the mantelpiece, tucked behind a small clock is a letter, with the seal broken. The room is in silence, but for the seconds ticking away. The clock, like the silver teapot is destined for the pawnbroker.

'Did Nicholas say when he's likely to return?' Suzanne Gregoire, or Gregory asks. Her auburn hair has come loose from the pins and combs and she puts up a hand to tuck a stray lock back in place. Her lovely face is discontented. She's not used to penury and uncertainty.

Her companion shrugs. The gesture should be one of Gallic charm: a raising and lowering of the shoulders, but today it looks more like defeat. 'He's in Amsterdam, and he doesn't say when he's coming back.'

'Do you trust him?'

'About as far as I can throw him,' Jeanne replies, flatly.

At the end of last year, the Assembly dropped the charges against Jeanne de la Motte and her husband, on a technicality. The leader, Mirabeau, sent an agent to meet with Nicholas, to secure the return of the remains of the diamonds to the jewellers. Neither Nicholas nor Jeanne de la Motte trusted the messenger, and two days after the offer of a conditional pardon was made, Nicholas took ship for Russia, to seek a buyer for what remained of the notorious Boehmer and Bessange necklace. He's been travelling around Europe and his wife is certain he won't be returning to her.

Jeanne de la Motte wears her fichu higher over her right breast. The fabric conceals the ugly brand on her flesh- the letter V for robber and the fleur de lis are burned into both shoulders and her bosom. Her accomplices in the swindle were exiled, but the King, furious at how the scandal had harmed his wife, insisted that Jeanne alone be imprisoned and branded. 'I would still be in the Salpetriere without your help, Suzanne. I cannot go back while that woman lives.' Her bitterness towards Queen Marie Antoinette is a festering sore.

Women of the Revolution

Suzanne looks down at her hands. These two have been friends from childhood. Both are orphans, whose education was paid by charitable patrons. They attended school at Passy; were sent to the convent at Longchamps; both married the first man they could persuade into wedlock to avoid the life of a nun. Now, they have been tricked by their husbands. Nicholas tours Europe, fencing diamonds and pearls from the necklace. His wife hasn't seen a penny and lives off the sales of her memoirs. Since last year, her notoriety, which made her the toast of London for a few weeks, has fallen out of fashion. As for Suzanne, Gregoire, the half Irish, half French deputy, alarmed by reports of the ferocity of his wife's attack on the Queen's bedchamber, tried to lock her away in the Charenton asylum. She escaped by the skin of her teeth, aided by printer and pamphleteer, Le Maitre. Now, even Le Maitre has deserted them, scurrying back to France.

They miss the maid, who always ensured their linen was washed and their gowns freshened. Despite copious applications of cologne, Suzanne doesn't feel clean. There's a grubby stain on Jeanne's dressing robe, and they have stopped powdering their hair, because brushing it out takes so long. They take it in turns to fetch water from the butt outside the scullery, hauling the precious pail up four flights of stairs.

'Do you have any money left, Suzanne?'

Suzanne shakes her head. She received three large diamonds from the necklace, shortly after it fell into the hands of the La Mottes, and had them placed into a silver filigree brooch, until the time was right to sell them. She told anyone who admired them that they were paste. They were hidden in plain sight in a trinket box in her bureau in the house at Versailles and she insisted Le Maitre took her there to retrieve the pin on their flight to England. In the confusion after the Women's March last October, the house was unlocked- the door wide open. The jewels were gone. She arrived in London with only the clothes on her back and a small purse of coin and sought out her old friend, only to learn that Jeanne was equally poor.

The two women have spent months living on their wits. Now, as French court emigres loyal to King Louis XVI arrive, with tales of the Revolution, they are finding doors slammed in their faces.

Only weeks ago, they dined with politicians like Fox and Pitt. They were invited to visit the Prince of Wales and his mistress at Brighton. Whenever Jeanne de la Motte appeared in society, with copies of her memoirs, she seldom returned to the lodging with empty pockets. Yesterday, they attended a theatrical performance, and had rotten fruit thrown at them as they walked home through Covent Garden. The words that accompanied the missiles were even worse.

It might have been different. Suzanne's plan to reunite Ottilie, the Queen's disgraced favourite with her husband, Gianfranco Valenti and their daughter Lucette in public had almost worked. Valenti, released from the Bastille was living under her roof, and she had the daughter safely stowed in the farm at the Hameau. All she needed was the location of Ottilie. Once all three were together, she planned to use their story to denounce the behaviour of the Queen. It was a perfect way to rouse the mob: the scandal of a family parted by Court intrigue. Le Maitre, her fellow conspirator, agreed it would further the case for Philippe, the King's cousin, to replace Louis as a constitutional monarch.

Suzanne used a young Scottish agent provocateur, Jacques, to lure the daughter into a trap. Under Suzanne's spell, he also revealed his twin sister had taken his place as clerk to the Usher of the Assembly. Jacob Rose had sent her to Longchamps on a mission to locate the girl and her mother and on her return, Suzanne kidnapped her, locking her in a rat- infested attic, to make her talk. Before the girl cracked, there was a stirring in the streets, and they set out on the March to Versailles, to put a stop to the King's distance from his people.

Those two days were a triumph- if a bloody one. Suzanne had never felt so alive, or so powerful- but once they returned to Paris, it fell apart.

She blames Mirabeau for pouring poison in her husband's ear. And she blames Jacob Alexander Rose and his cross-dressing clerk even more.

Chapter 2

February, 1790
Paris

Jean the clerk perches at Jacob's old desk in the ground floor room with the ledgers in front of her. It's taken some persuasion to convince Jacob to let her resume her disguise as a lad. It has come down to practicality. As a woman of the bourgeoisie, she would be an incumbrance. She could go nowhere without a male escort. She would not be permitted to continue as a notary's clerk. Jacob would have to either send her back to Scotland, acquire lodgings for her in a convent, or move to a larger house with servants, and make her his housekeeper. He cannot afford to lose an assistant he trusts, nor does he want to have a household who might spy on him.

It isn't a hardship for Jean, who knows she has neither beauty nor fortune to attract a husband. Her mousy brown hair and slightly protuberant blue grey eyes, and her slight figure look better as a boy. All she has ever wanted is an education, and back in Scotland, she took advantage of her twin brother's laziness to attend lectures at Aberdeen University in his place, dressed in his old clothing. Here, she has access to Jacob Rose' law books and a pass that gives her the right to study in the library of Scots College in the Rue Ecosse. The work of a notary's clerk keeps her mind occupied, and she is freed from those ladylike skills of needlework, which she detests.

Jacob spends his days at the Assembly, and most evenings on his return he dines and repairs to his bedchamber to transcribe his notes and write reports and letters. Once a week he might take her with him to visit the Geddes couple, and he leaves her to Francine, while he talks with Sandy about Scottish matters. Francine is one of the few who know her secret, and she has been sworn to silence. It is thanks to Francine that a tailor made her a suit of clothes that fit better than her father's old garb, and that she looks less of a downtrodden dogsbody and more like an aspiring notary's clerk.

Jacob takes great care to keep his bedchamber locked, and with a pang of guilt she remembers her twin brother's skeleton key and how he broke in and opened Jacob's desk to read the reports. Johnny- who now goes by the name of Jacques- vanished after she helped herself to his clothes in that house in Versailles. She knows he won't be far away- sometimes, she catches a glimpse out of the corner of her eye. He's kept his hair short, and his clothing is dark, and nondescript. She knows he's working with Marat. She's seen the scandal sheets and the political diatribes he churns out on that printing press. She knows the trouble he can cause. The Paris police ordered Marat's arrest in January, after he published a furious attack on Necker, the finance minister. The sans culottes from the Cordeliers quarter fought off the municipal police, and Marat escaped. Rumour has it that he's in London, headed for friends from his days in Scotland. She can only hope that he's taken her brother with him.

On his most recent voyage, Cargill's cart bore a piece of furniture- a cabinet, sent from Jacob's cousin George. It took Cargill, Jacob and herself to manoeuvre it up the stairs to Jacob's bedchamber, where it sits in the corner. 'Your brother's wee keys won't work on this,' Cargill told her. 'It's the work of Willie Brodie- the man they called the Deacon. He put in secret drawers that would defy burglars- given he was one himself, he knew what he was doing. George got the Kilravock men to buy it from his widow, and thought it might come in handy for you, Jacob.'

Security is important. Jacob might be an official rather than a member of the Assembly, but he's been watched by all manner of men- and women- who take a close interest in his position and his access to men like Mirabeau. It would take very little to place him in the way of danger, and in turn, she would also be vulnerable. She's told him not to share the secret of the cabinet, lest her brother attempt his old tricks. Instead, some information- of a less serious nature, is locked in the downstairs desk. Let Johnny think he's a skilled spy- this way they can decide what Le Maitre or Marat can see.

CHAPTER 3

Jacob is a man of habit and routine. He starts his day early, washing and shaving in a single bowl of hot water, before breakfasting lightly on coffee and porridge and walking to the Assembly, his cane always in one hand and a leather satchel containing the essential papers slung across his body. Before he leaves the house, he entrusts his clerk with papers which must be sent to Scotland through Sandy Geddes in crates of household goods. His day at the Assembly requires his full concentration. The discourse, since the Women's March has grown increasingly radical.

In his early thirties, he is neither handsome nor ill favoured; neither tall nor short. He wears his thick brown hair tied at the nape of his neck, dresses in the sombre dark colours of the legal profession and carries a cane with a concealed sword, which he knows how to use. There's a fierce intelligence in his eyes, although as an Usher of the Assembly rather than a deputy, if he has ideas, he must keep them to himself or offer them through others, like his friend Mirabeau.

He enjoys his daily walks. They offer moments of

contemplation away from the debating chamber and the nighttime correspondence. In the noisy, cheerful morning market, where Parisians mingle with countrymen selling cheeses and vegetables, he passes shopkeepers and stall holders he has known for many years, who regard him as an amiable acquaintance, and as a Scot, something of an oddity. At one stall, he buys a rosy apple and some Normandie cheese which he stows in his pockets for his lunch. He rarely has time to dine with the deputies and must ensure the records of the morning are accurate. At another stall he purchases a copy of the Universal Monitor- a newspaper he trusts to document the proceedings of the previous day's Assembly business, without the histrionics of Marat's People's Friend.

The market allows him to listen to what ordinary people think of what is going on, and he often picks up titbits of scandal. One stall keeper tells of an inn where card sharps cheat people out of their hard-earned money. Another tells of attacks on unlit streets and asks what the Assembly plans to do to protect ordinary citizens?

Today, there is a commotion by the river. The Seine, as usual, is busy with boats carrying goods, and passengers. Smaller vessels are tied up and among these, a boatman is deploying his hook to gather in a body. There's nothing unusual about that. Jacob's seen more than his share of drunks pulled out of the water, poor souls who lost their footing after too many cups of wine and a walk home on a moonless night.

There's something different about this one. The boatman hollers for attention, and the other river men gather round. Jacob pulls his silver watch from his pocket, consults the time, and is about to make haste, when the officers of the Mare Chaussee arrive. He will no doubt be asked about this incident, so he draws closer.

Women of the Revolution

The body is bloated: gases inside it have propelled it to the surface. 'How long do you think it's been in there?' asks a tall, thin official, delicately holding a handkerchief to his face.

The boatman replies, 'Not long – if it was in there for three weeks, it would be almost black. This one's just turning green.'

'So, days rather than weeks?' The second official – almost a head shorter than his fellow and almost twice his girth- is more practical and leans over to take a better look at the corpse, which has now been landed like a monstrous fish, laid out on the riverbank.

Jacob watches as the body is lifted onto a stretcher and placed on a cart, to be taken to the new Paris Morgue, as is the case for any corpse recovered from the Seine, and anyone unclaimed by family.

The officials are asking questions of the boatman. 'Did you find a coat? Shoes? Anything to tell us who he is?' The boatman shrugs.

'He washed up here, but there's no saying where he went into the water. The current's running downstream and there's been heavy rain this last fortnight. He could have fallen in anywhere.'

Jacob coughs gently to get their attention. 'I am Jacob Rose, Usher to the Assembly. I saw this poor soul pulled out of the river shortly before you arrived. I can confirm that what you see is all that was to be found here.' His voice and demeanour command the respect of the officials, in a way that the boatman did not.

He casts an eye over the remains. There's no coat, or shoes, but the quality of the knee breeches and stockings suggest this was no peasant. The lace on the shirt cuffs and stock might have been nibbled by the fishes, but they are what he's seen worn by the wealthier members of the

Assembly. He's also noticed sharp slashes in the fabric, tinged with faded bloodstains. These might have been inflicted by the body being caught on the hull of a boat, but Jacob has another theory.

'It looks as if this man took his coat off to fight a duel. Those look like slashes from a rapier. Can you find a surgeon to look at him?'

He can see their initial respect turning to irritation. They are not used to being told how to do their job. The boatman, turning back to stow his grappling hook, is grinning.

'Rather late for that,' the taller official snaps.

'That may well be- but this man needs to be identified and kept ready for his people to claim him.' Jacob gives a brief salute and resumes his walk to work.

Chapter 4

The Assembly declares war on the Church. It is inevitable that after centuries of influence, that its wealth and landholdings should come under scrutiny. There's no Richelieu or Mazarin wielding power these days and hasn't been since the Sun King built Versailles and seduced the Court to its gilded halls. Rohan, the last Cardinal courtier was caught up in the affair of the Diamond Necklace and shown to be a venal idiot. So why should the Church hang on to its extensive property when the State coffers are so empty? The Church pays no taxes and thrives while the people starve.

Even Mirabeau and the nobles agree, but it will be the lawyers- notaries like Jacob Rose who will be faced with the mountain of administration that sequestration involves.

Henry VIII of England had the wily Cromwell to facilitate his land grab. In his day, there were still peasants who clung to the old faith, often fighting the King's guard to defend the relics and paying with their lives. France, however, is being practical, and no villager who has gone hungry while the priests and bishops dined well, will disagree, other than a handful of zealots in the south. The church lands will be sold through municipalities or held by them and there is talk of a new currency- the Assignat- linked to the value of the property. In this new age of reason and enlightenment, it can be argued that the place of religion is fading. Nobody is suggesting a complete ban- but now parish priests must read aloud the decrees of the Assembly from the pulpit, and nobody is to take religious vows.

Of greater concern is the suppression of religious orders. Where will the plainer, younger and unmarried daughters be sent by their parents now, if there are no convents to take them in, one bishop asks. Many such places these days are little more than boarding houses for gentlewomen abandoned by husbands and family. The convents and abbeys are often refuges for women of gentle birth fleeing a violent spouse. A convent is often the only place a woman can seek an education, after all. Jacob thinks of his clerk, who was prepared to risk discovery to attend Aberdeen University lectures in her brother's place. Surely it is time for the Rights of Woman?

He seeks out a messenger and tells him of the morning's incident by the river. He sends a note to the morgue, requesting to be informed of the identity of the victim, and does not expect a response. Duelling might have been outlawed by Edicts of the Sun King, but it continues, and officials turn a blind eye, unless those fighting are prominent enough for there to be consternation if one of them should be killed. Besides, since last October, members of the Royal Court have been slipping quietly away, including the King's maiden aunts. Unless someone reports this man missing, they might never discover who he is.

He is clearing his desk at the end of the day when the official returns, bearing a reply. He is invited to call at the Paris Morgue on his way home. There has been a development. He sighs. He was looking forward to a quiet dinner at an inn, with a glass of red, and the company of his clerk, but his curiosity gets the better of him. He gathers up his papers, calls for his coat, hat and cane, and sets out on the detour that will take him out of his way home.

Chapter 5

The limewashed walls of the Paris Morgue reflect the glow from the candles in paired sconces with glass shades. The floor is stone and has been recently washed. It is clean, functional and completely stripped back.

The surgeon, Felix Vicq d'Azyr -has finished his examination. Jacob respects and admires him. He's put forward plans to the Assembly to transform the teaching of medicine. 'It needs to be in the hands of scientists- not quacks like that scoundrel Marat. After all, if we can inoculate against smallpox, just think what we could do if we stopped bleeding every sick person whether they needed it or not and desist from offering laudanum for every ailment?' He has his coat on and apologises that he has a patient to see and cannot stay. However, he hands Jacob his report and introduces the two people standing by the corpse on its marble bier.

John Christophe Curtius is Swiss, trained in medicine, but Jacob knows of him as the maker of wax likenesses of notable people. Jean had watched as two of the busts- D'Orleans and Necker were paraded at the Palais Royal the day before the Bastille fell. Curtius introduces the capable young woman whose gown is fully hidden under a voluminous smock as his niece, Marie Grosholtz. They began their careers dissecting bodies to create wax models to instruct medical students. Their more recent work together entertains the public in their exhibition at the Palais Royal and at the grisly Chamber of Horrors at Boulevard du Temple. However, they are frequently called to document those bodies brought to the Morgue from the river, especially if they are too far gone for identification by family.

The body has been stripped and the garments are neatly laid out on a table. Curtius indicates the lines of neat stitching where the surgeon has opened the body. 'He did not die by drowning,' he explains, pointing to the neck. 'There is a ligature mark on the throat, and judging by the slashes to the arms- which are deeper than we might expect from a duel, we can assume he lost a good deal of blood. The shirt was soaked, and the gore diluted, which made drowning appear the more obvious death.'

Jacob pinches the bridge of his nose and takes a deep breath. His cleared sinuses are assailed by chemicals and the smell of decay.

'Might the duel have been interrupted and this poor devil robbed and strangled?' he asks.

'That is a possibility,' Curtius replies. 'In a duel, he would have removed his coat and handed it to his second, but unless we can find the second, the opponent and the location where he died, we cannot confirm that. We assume he wore a court wig and took that off before the affray. His hair is kept much shorter than usual. Marie, here. will assist me in making a death mask, which may be used to help identification. After that, we shall embalm the body, keep it cold and place it ready for burial.'

Marie has her materials to hand, and Jacob understands

that the process will not proceed until he has left. The grisly task is the last thing a young woman should be doing, but she is focused and calm, and has obviously done such things many times before.

'Is there anything else we should note?' he asks.

Marie nods. 'I believe this gentleman is of mixed race, and that he came from the Caribbean islands.' She indicates the corpse' hair, which is close cropped, but has tight curls, and his skin. 'Putrefaction is setting in, but this man was used to being in a hot climate. He's not African, but I suspect one of his grandparents might have been. He's not a working man- his fingernails are too well manicured for that.' She turns and touches the shirt. 'The cotton for this is from the Americas, not Egypt- it is a longer staple, and spun in an English mill, not a French one. The lace is Honiton, not Brussels.'

'Not a courtier, then?' Jacob murmurs.

She shakes her head. 'His garments are fine- but they are not French. Perhaps he is a diplomat? Try the foreign embassies to see if anyone is missing?' she suggests.

Jacob picks up the breeches. 'These do not offer up any clues?' He takes spectacles from his pocket and peers at the cloth. There are two buttons and they do not match. He asks her to look. 'These are silver, but one of them has a crest.'

Marie turns to the desk, takes a stick of sealing wax, heats it over a candle and lets the dark red substance drip onto parchment before dipping the button into it, taking an impression.

'If you can locate the owner of this crest, you might also discover who this poor soul really is.'

Chapter 6

It is after eight when Jacob arrives home and Jean the clerk is waiting for him with a worried frown, and a tray laden with a bowl and a hunk of bread and cheese. There is soup in the blackened iron pan hanging over the fire and once he has taken off his warm greatcoat and hat, and rubbed his hands vigorously, she ladles the heated broth into the bowl and watches him eat. Cooking is not her strength, but she can't go far wrong with broth. Normally, they would eat in the nearest inn, but when he's delayed, she scratches together a supper of sorts. When he's finished and wiped the bowl clean with the last of the bread, she puts the tea kettle ready and hands him the caddy.

She tells him she ate earlier, when she delivered a document to Mercier, the draper. He has a cousin living with him from the country who is an excellent cook, and no doubt will be a capable housekeeper.

'We had roasted fowl, and she gave me some of the bones and a bit of her stock to take home. I used it for the soup.' He opens the caddy, using the key from his chain and spoons the precious leaves into the warmed silver teapot, pouring the hot water over it. The cups and saucers stand ready, and Jean slices a hunk of butter cake- another gift from the Mercier household -into several pieces.

He accepts a slice and bites into it gratefully, almost groaning with delight at the richness of it. 'Is the cousin beautiful as well as talented?' he asks.

She grins- 'Fair, fat and forty, and very bossy.'

He tells her about the events of the day and of his meeting with Marie Grosholtz at the morgue. 'You've seen some of their work, haven't you?" he asks.

She shudders. 'Those wax figures at the Palais Royal? They put me in mind of beheadings. They were so true to life.' She was present at the demonstration outside the Palais Royal last July and the memory of a woman torn apart for speaking in favour of the King still haunts her.

She's curious about the body from the river, and he hands over the wax with the impression from the button. She holds it to the light, taking care not to let it touch the candles, and takes a magnifying glass to examine the markings.

'If I tasked you with finding the owner of the crest, how would you go about it?' he asks.

She turns the seal over in her fingers. 'First, I'd ask Mercier about who makes or engraves the buttons. I could get Francine to ask her sister if she knows the crest?'

'And if the owner is from another country?'

'If he's British, could Cargill find out? Or your cousin George?'

She paces the room, stops and turns. 'Two buttons, only one of which had this crest? Perhaps a button was lost and the tailor who mended it had to supply another one, which was plain?'

'Isn't that a needle in a haystack?' Jacob asks.

'Not necessarily. If the dead man had been at Court, the

chances are that the repair would have been done at Versailles, and Mercier's brother might have supplied the replacement. He would know the menders, and I could get a list from him.' She pauses, 'He's visiting his brother this week. I can call on them and ask him.' There's a smile playing on her lips.

'Might that involve another excuse for some Mercier hospitality?' he suggests.

'I hear the cousin makes an excellent Tarte Tatin. Besides, it will let me see our old friend Jules and get news of Lucette.'

'Then I shall leave this in your capable hands, Jean.'

'Are you working this evening? Do you need me to transcribe notes?' she asks. 'I've lit the fire in your room. It should be warm.' He sees her glance flicker to the novel on the desk, which she had been reading before he arrived home.

He thanks her and taking a candle from the mantelpiece, he climbs the stairs, leaving her to sit by the fire with Fanny Burney's *Evelina*.

CHAPTER 7

March, 1790
London

Cheapside's Gutter Lane was originally called Godrun's Lane. Over the centuries, it's assumed its more colloquial title, and anyone looking for a saddle maker or small goods craftsman will find it here.

It is also an area frequented by those in need of a pawnbroker, and the day has come for the ladies of the attic to liquidate their last assets. Suzanne and Jeanne de la Motte have spent the past month living on their wits and keeping out of their landlord's way.

They stand in a dark and frowsy shop that reeks of the ancient tabby cat who lounges on the counter. They empty the drawstring bag that Suzanne carries under her cloak, in case of footpads. The items, laid out on the counter, are a dismal set of worldly goods. The tarnished silver tea pot; milk and sugar set; a few pieces of paste jewellery and three spoons, along with the set of combs Jeanne de la Motte wore in her hair when she was thrown into prison, won't fetch much.

Last night Jeanne suggested selling their teeth- but Suzanne snapped, 'I'd sooner sell my body.' She's seen poor souls submit to the pliers and the prospect of losing her looks does not appeal.

'It might come to that. Then we'd both be in the gutter.'

The elderly woman behind the counter hasn't seen a good wash for weeks, Suzanne suspects, and she probably shares her bed with that cat and a selection of fleas. It is hard to tell if her hair is powdered or naturally white, and it's thinning in places. She wears mittens on her hands, as she sorts through the little horde. She offers a sum so low; Suzanne immediately turns it down.

'Please yourself,' the crone replies, 'Beggars can't be choosers.'

Suzanne is about to sweep the items off the counter, when Jeanne squeezes her shoulder. 'I've had an idea. We can get a better price for the silver elsewhere. Take what she offers for the trinkets.'

Across the road is the small shop of a button maker. It looks more respectable than the pawnbroker's- it's had a recent coat of paint and the pavement outside has been swept. In the window is a tray of small silver goods- shoe buckles, snuff boxes buttons and combs. There's a sign in the window: Help wanted.

They open the door and a bell tinkles, alerting the owner to the presence of customers. The man is in his forties, with thick light brown hair pulled back into a queue and he wears a leather apron over his shirt and knee breeches. He rushes forward, bowing to them. Suzanne reflects they must still look like ladies of quality.

'I am at your service, ladies. How might I be of assistance?'

Jeanne points at the sign in the window. 'I think it might

be a case of how we might be of assistance to you?'

They must not appear to be too desperate, Suzanne thinks, as her friend explains they are French emigres, fleeing the dreadful Revolutionaries, and separated from all their worldly goods for the time being. They seek respectable employment and a place to live simply, until their own country returns to its senses. They do not give their real names.

Jeanne has some skill as an engraver and polisher, she explains, while her friend knows their fellow emigres and can sell buttons and other goods to them.

He looks doubtful, but he's obviously considering their suggestion. The shop belonged to his late parents. His mother was a button maker to the quality- a buckle maker and a goldsmith too. Alas, they are gone, and while he can produce the plainer goods, he lacks a salesperson and could do with a workshop assistant. There's a room in his home- on the floor above, which he sometimes rents out. It won't be what they are used to, but he will offer a fortnight's trial to see how they get on.

They agree and return to their lodgings, to retrieve what's left of their belongings, allow Jeanne to forge a letter of recommendation and depart- without paying their bill.

Their new home is tiny- the whitewashed room is just big enough to contain the small bed they will have to share- along with a washstand and two stools. 'Are you mad?' Suzanne asks Jeanne.

'I saw Marat looking in the window while we were in the pawnbroker,' she replies. 'He's rubbed the Assembly up the wrong way and run back to England. All we need to do is to find him and who is helping him here- and see if they can reach out a hand to two gentlewomen in need. I'm buying us time, Suzanne. Now you can do your part and make yourself useful. It's this or the streets, and if it's all the same to you,

Women of the Revolution

I'm going to settle for a roof over my head and a hot meal every day.

Chapter 8

March, 1790
Paris

Mercier takes the sealing wax impression from Jean and squints at it in the light from the window. 'You say it was a silver button?' He moves it one way then another but shakes his head.

Jean says, 'I didn't see it, but Jacob did- in the Morgue. The assistant made this impression. There were two buttons- one was plain silver and the other had this marking. Is it some sort of family crest?'

Mercier shrugs. 'It's hard to tell, without seeing the original. It's unusual though. There's no heraldic shield or initials- only a tree with a hound at its foot. I shall ask Eugene.'

Jean follows him out of the shop, and through the small courtyard at the back to his home, where the cousin prepares lunch and his brother, proprietor of the Versailles branch of Mercier's, is consulting the stock sheets.

The Women's March resulted in the Royal Family being

forced to the Tuileries Palace, taking the court with them. Most aristocrats with rooms at Versailles had their own houses in the town of Versailles, and some choose to remain there, out of sight. Others return to their country estates, and some have taken themselves into exile. With their customers in disarray, the Mercier brothers must decide how their business continues- and how much of the stock to move to the smaller Paris premises.

Eugene Mercier produces a magnifying glass and looks at the piece of sealing wax. 'I've not seen this before, but you mentioned a plain silver button? Yes?'

Jean nods. 'There were two buttons- one plain silver and the other silver engraved with this device.'

'There I can assist you,' he smiles. His front teeth are stained- he is overfond of coffee and sweet biscuits. 'I supply plain silver buttons from England to Monsieur Chalonnier at Versailles. He arranges repairs to be done by piece workers and by tailors in Paris. Perhaps one of those might have worked on the garment?'

Jean agrees that yes, this is a possibility. Where might she find Chalonnier? This is turning into that very needle in the haystack. He scribbles an address, and she takes the piece of paper- and accepts the cousin's invitation to lunch. Outside, Jules the coachman is unloading bales of fabric from the conveyance, carrying each, wrapped in muslin, into the shop. She waves to her old friend- the former innkeeper and reminds herself to ask after his wife and Lucette, the daughter she was sent to find in those dramatic days of last year.

Lunch is delicious- the cousin presides over a spread of soup, salad and the Tarte Tatin, and prattles about a nephew who has applied for a commission in the army. The Assembly last month abolished the requirement for military officers to be solely from the nobility. Her brother-in-law is a deputy from the provinces, a man of worth, and can afford to support his son's ambitions.

'How long are you staying?' Jean asks.

'I am here until Easter, then I shall go to keep my sister company in Nancy. She has such a lovely house, and I look forward to helping with her herb garden. I do miss my own little cottage, but it is good to be needed.'

She presses another slice of tart on Jean- 'You young men need feeding up- you are far too thin.' Is this what having a mother would be like? Jean doesn't remember such kindness.

The cousin is a widow, of slender means who depends on the benevolence of relatives for a roof over her head. Perhaps she feels it necessary to praise and flatter, to keep on the right side of her hosts?

Jean greets Jules on her way out. He's looking tired, and she asks after his health and that of his wife. He tells her that they are well but lowers his voice to say that the Mercier's are letting some of their shop staff go, and that they worry they might also be surplus to requirements soon.

'Is Lucette still staying with you?' she asks.

He shakes his head. 'Lucette has employment with some ladies who are resident at Pentement Abbey. She's very fortunate and hopes to train as a ladies' maid.'

Jean offers her very best wishes to Lucette and asks to be reminded kindly to Jules' wife.

Jean turns to go, but before she can do so, he says, 'I hear Le Maitre is back from England, but Marat has taken his assistant- young Jacques- to London with him. It might be useful for your employer to know that.' He gives a faint smile, which she returns in kind.

Chapter 9

April, 1790
Arbroath, Scotland

Lorna Cargill follows her mother and sister through the side gate and into the Abbey graveyard. They tread carefully, past overgrown weeds interspersed with ancient tombstones- those of long dead monks and those others whose families have nobody left to remember them. Lorna doesn't much like the place, but her mother, Jessamine, insists on both daughters accompanying her on this weekly ritual. Their younger brother, Stephen, escorts them from the house to the Abbey and then sets off for his school, along the road.

The objective of the weekly visit is to lay flowers on the grave of Jessamine's grandmother: an old dragon of a woman who looked down on her daughter for marrying into trade. She'd been raised in a castle and came from landed gentry. She never let anyone forget that- especially her son in law.

The Cargill ladies reach the lair- a grand sandstone crown edifice. It's already begun to soften and crumble at the corners. Jessamine gives her instructions, which the girls can already recite from memory. The younger girl, Catherine is to fetch water from the well, while Lorna collects last week's posy and transfers it to the grave of Bella Sim, a neighbour whose son is at sea with Lorna's father and has no wife to tend his mother's grave.

Jessamine fusses over the flowers she has picked from her mother's walled garden that same morning. When the vase is filled with water, she arranges the cut daffodils and stands back, smoothing down her full skirts, straightening her fichu.

'Run along girls and see to Nanny and Billy.' It was her father's idea to keep a small herd of goats tethered in the Abbey grounds to keep down the grass and weeds. A makeshift fence separates the graveyard from the cloisters, but Nanny enjoys a snack of flowers and constantly knocks it over.

The girls in their muslin gowns and straw bonnets are in the fashion embraced by the French queen – shepherdesses, but their muslin costs a guinea a length- well beyond the pocket of any real farm worker.

Jessamine turns her attention to the real purpose of her visit, walking through the archway to the side of the Round O- the landmark that Andrew looks for to guide his ship into port. She glances up at the old Abbey guesthouse and opens the door opposite to enter the Abbot's House.

The thread factory is working at full tilt, but she goes to the Abbot's study, closing the door behind her. Her father, in shirtsleeves, is expecting her. He's lit the fire and the kettle on a chain over the flames has reached a rolling boil, spluttering steam. The teapot, caddy and two delicate porcelain cups and deep saucers stand ready for Jessamine's ministrations.

'Good day to you, faither. Shall I mak the tea?' she asks.

'Aye, Jessie, that would be grand. Nae too strong, mind.'

Women of the Revolution

The lapse into Scots indicates he's in a good mood. She doesn't know how long that mood will last, especially when she gives him the letters that arrived last night.

The ledgers stand ready on the desk. Mid-morning tea, once a week, is a ritual that everyone knows about- the excuse for her visits. Until fifteen years ago, Jessamine's brother, William, was their father's heir. A fine young man, educated in Latin and Greek, with a degree from the University of St Andrews. He had a good head for business and his father reckoned the family business would thrive under his stewardship. Even the old dragon doted on Will, saying he might almost pass for gentry.

He'd wanted a commission in the Army and to see a bit of the world, but his father stood firm against that, insisting he was needed in the firm.

The clacking of the machinery, even through the firmly closed door, always makes Jessamine's hand shake a little.

The accident- down the road in the Mill- didn't seem a danger to life at first, but the cut to the young master's hand became infected. Despite leeches and maggots, and powders, the infection raged through his body. She still recalls the screams through the gag when his arm was amputated to the elbow.

When William died in his father's arms, something broke in every one of the family.

She was already twenty-two, and on the shelf, attending occasional parties where she sat with the other wallflowers, making polite conversation with curates and chaperones, while the pretty girls danced with the eligible young men.

A mill owner without a son. Grieving parents who had hardly given their plain daughter a second thought, other than finding her useful about the house.

Her brother's friend Andrew was home from the sea and helped to carry the coffin at William's funeral. The faithful, solid soul was at her side in the dark days that followed.

Theirs wasn't a love match, but it has become a strong marriage. As a single woman, Jess could only inherit under the control of Trustees. As a married woman, she isn't entitled to hold property in her own right, but with a husband who knows his place, the family fortunes are in safe hands.

Her father bought Andrew with a ship- the Lady Jessamine. It meant he could leave his family's cargo fleet for a tall ship that can navigate the Atlantic for trade with the former colonies and the French controlled islands. It's added to their wealth, and once a week, Jessamine and her father take tea and go through the books. She already understands the nature of the work and could take charge, if required to do so.

She hands her father his cup and he pours the tea into the deep saucer to let it cool for a minute before transferring it back to the cup and thence to his lips. The cup is delicate and will crack if he drinks straight from it. She does likewise, and sips slowly, savouring the smoky aroma. Tea from China is her vice, but she notices the flagon on the desk, half full. She knows her father drinks excessively of late. Her mother is tight lipped at the dinner table when he's imbibed too much.

He's easily irritated in his cups, although seldom with her. Lately, though, he's taken against Andrew, complaining he's spending too little time at home.

'You can't have it both ways, faither. You need him at sea for the trade.'

The trade with France – delivering documents, passengers and woollen cloth, returning with wine, brandy and silk- is lucrative. Her house at Market Gate is furnished with fine pieces and rugs. The cups in their hands come from the works at Sevres- delivered by Andrew from a previous voyage. The carriage of the Osnaburg cloth across the ocean, where he's gone for months rather than weeks is another matter. Her husband snaps at her father when he's home from those trips. She looks down from the window. Each window in the thread factory has forty-eight pieces of glass, held in place with lead strips that cast shadowed lattices on the whitewashed wall in the sunshine. Young Catherine, her middle child, is playing with a baby goat. Her fair hair has escaped her bonnet, and she looks carefree and pretty. Jessamine is fond of her daughters, but Stephen, her youngest is her real prize. It will be he who secures the family's future.

When she unpacked the Sevres cups, she found French pamphlets tucked in beside them in the straw wadding. They were typical of the stuff coming from France of late- radicals and revolutionaries- and had they been seen by Customs, they'd have been confiscated and Andrew would have been in trouble. Jessamine shared the French lessons with her brother and can translate, even though it takes a long time to remember the words. One pamphlet, by a woman called Olympe des Gouges, echoed what Mr Wilberforce has been saying in the Courant- that slavery is wrong and the slave trade must be stopped.

When she told her husband of her concern at this sudden interest in politics, he reminded her where her father's money came from. 'Every entry in your balance sheets comes from selling cloth to slave owners, who have the power of life and death over those poor souls. Can you live with that? I'm not so sure I can.'

'Besides,' he continues, 'that writer has other notions, like asking people what sort of government they want, and letting women have rights. I'm sure you'd agree with those.'

Chapter 10

April, 1790
Paris

A night at the theatre is a rare treat for Jean the clerk. Sandy Geddes secured a row of the cheaper seats, and the Scots in Paris are making an evening of it. They've started their Saturday festivities at a fashionable restaurant, where the chef is a celebrity, whose appearance after dessert is applauded even by members of the Court. Jean hired a finer coat for the evening and has a lace edged stock kept well tucked in for fear of getting a dab of sauce on it.

The theatre is a modest building, little larger than a church hall, with a stage draped in shabby velvet, and lit by candles, reflected in mirrored sconces. These establishments pop-up across Paris- and many burn down just as quickly- the candles and whale oil lamps are fire hazards.

The programme is an interesting one, Francine Geddes explains, because there is to be a one act play by Philippe Egalite's friend, Olympe des Gouges. She's known for her campaigning zeal over everything from improving roads to her wish to abolish slavery. Tonight, the Marquise and her black page, Etienne, are tactfully not invited to be in their company.

The second half of the programme is a rare appearance by Philippe's friend and protegee, the Chevalier de Saint Georges, with one of his shorter compositions for the orchestra. The Chevalier, Joseph Bologna, is the son of a plantation owner and a former slave. It is said that he is turning his back on music to raise a regiment of black soldiers. His mother, Nanon, sits near the Scottish party, fanning herself with her programme, eyes glued to the stage. The decision in the Assembly last month not to abolish slavery has been a blow to Bologna and his mother and to Olympe des Gouges. The islands might be allowed their own assemblies- but the enslaved are no closer to freedom. This evening was planned several months ago, before the debate in the Assembly. Philippe himself is in England, sent on an errand to get him out of the country. Everyone knows the King might accept the Assembly in public, but in private he plots and schemes to attempt to restore his power. The Queen, after all, is sister to the emperor and Louis' aunts are on good terms with the Holy See.

Jacob watches the Chevalier as his bow – pausing for a second with an air of anticipation -electrifies the air. The melody speaks to every soul, tingling even Jacob's spine. His clerk is transfixed, oblivious to everyone else around, leaning forward on the uncomfortable seat, tapping a finger in time to the tune. Of course, he reflects, there's been precious little music in Jean's life. The clergyman she and her twin stayed with believed music was sinful, if it wasn't psalms.

The playwright sits in a makeshift box to one side of the stage. She's discreetly scanning the audience, looking for the more influential patrons. She's well dressed, if not in the most a la mode style. Francine whispers to Jacob, 'She's a widow- has been since her son was a year old. She has a lover- but she refuses to marry again. She says marriage gives men too much power over their wives.'

Jacob smiles. 'Didn't she write that marriage is the tomb of trust and love?'

'I should have known you'd have read her work,' Francine replies. 'When do you have the time? You always seem to be working!'

'I'm sent copies of all the latest plays and novels, and Jean reads them and points out the lines I should quote in society. If I appear well read, my clerk should take credit, also.'

Bologna reminds Jacob of the dead man at the Paris Morgue. He's well dressed, with the same striking physique- strong but graceful in proportion. Jacob wonders if he can speak with him after the curtain falls. Perhaps the mystery man may have been known to him? Possibly one of his soldiers?

Jean is lost in the music. Francine told her the stories of how Bologna captivated the Court when he was launched as a musician- a rival even to Mozart and to the Queen's former music master Gluck. 'He is proud, and arrogant, and he made the mistake of not flattering those harridans of divas. They refused to perform if he was made director of the Opera. He's never forgiven Marie Antoinette for giving in to them and handing the post to Gluck.'

There are too many grudges, Jean concludes. The French Royal Family squabble amongst themselves. The fights create factions. Philippe Egalite might sit in the Assembly, but he was the Duc de Chartres, and it was outside his Palais Royal that the mob set alight their grievances. Jean hasn't set eyes on him, other than the wax bust that was carried aloft during that first riot, but it is said that Le Maitre and the Gregory woman worked for him. Is it any surprise that he, like Suzanne Gregory, Marat and Jean's brother Jacques are all currently in England?

Jean has enjoyed this little holiday from work. The delicate flavours of the food; the intellectual stimulation of the play and the extraordinary music have all lifted her mood, but she's only too aware that even the happiest of days can be turned by politics— and this evening's performance has been all about those.

CHAPTER 11

Bologna and De Gouges hold a soiree in the backstage rooms at the end of the evening's entertainment. There is wine- a rather fine Sancerre from the Loire valley- and some cheese and fruit. They speak to their guests and admirers about their dismay at the slavery vote.

Olympe changed her name from plain Marie Aubry, widow of a caterer who drowned in floods, to the more patrician sounding de Gouges. She has a wealthy patron who allowed her to move from Occitan speaking Montauban to Paris, and she has published novels and had her work: a play condemning slavery - performed at the Comedie Francaise. 'Where hecklers ruined my production- hecklers paid by slave owners. That is why we must guard this theatre. I do not approve of violence, no matter what others might say about me.'

'Have you read the works of de Saint Mery?' the playwright asks Jacob and Sandy. 'He wrote a two-volume account of life on Saint Domingue, and you might find it enlightening.'

Jacob tells her that he has not but knows there are

deputies who used the contents to argue for the abolition of slavery.

She sighs. 'I suppose in the end it comes down to money. How many of our great houses grow rich from those plantations where half a million slaves toil under dreadful conditions?'

Sandy looks uncomfortable. Much of his trade is in sugar, coffee and cotton, as is the case with the merchants of Glasgow. His sister-in-law, Henriette is married to a nobleman whose family owns plantations. How can slavery be stopped when so many powerful men have so much to lose?

Close up, Olympe de Gouges is still beautiful, but the wisdom of middle age is etched in the fine lines around her eyes and mouth. She is eager to talk about her play, and Sandy and Francine are all too willing to listen. Jean lurks with intent beside them. She wants to ask about the work de Gouges is currently engaged upon- a treatise on the rights of woman.

Jacob has his eyes on Bologna, who has packed up his violin and seems eager to leave. 'I wonder if I might have a word with you, Chevalier?'

The moment he mentions the body at the Morgue, Bologna is visibly tense. He's as renowned for his swordsmanship as he is for his music, and it could easily turn out that he was the opponent in the duel against the dead man.

'I assure you, Sir, that I have fought no duels. I cannot afford to waste time on petty grievances when there are more important fights ahead of us. I have barely left this theatre for a fortnight- Madame des Gouges will confirm that. With those criminals who fire buildings at large, we thought it best to stay here, and we've slept in the tiring rooms.'

'I wondered if the dead man might have been one of your

regiment?' Jacob describes the corpse's attire and the two buttons in as much detail as he can. The wax impression is with Mercier's brother, who is making his own enquiries.

'A person of mixed race, you say?' The Chevalier shudders at the terms before he recovers his composure and raises his elegant eyebrows. 'I have none among my troops. Have you considered your dead man might be a servant and the button part of a livery?'

Jacob nods, 'The thought crossed my mind. Where would you suggest we should start looking?' He holds the Chevalier in his steady gaze- and notes the man does not flinch or look away.

'I am afraid I cannot help you, sir.' He pauses, then as if the thought has struck him, 'You might wish to speak to those who come from the islands? They keep to themselves, but you might visit the Abbey at Pentemont? Some ladies from the islands live there. They might recognise the crest.'

Chapter 12

After weeks of letter writing, Chalonnier agrees to see Jacob. He has business in Paris and is delighted to accept a dinner at the Geddes house. He is much too important to bother with a mere clerk, but the Usher has well connected friends. With so many leaving Versailles, his business needs new clients and the members of the Assembly require clothing and valeting, don't they?

Auguste Chalonnier is an oddity. He is of medium height and very slight build, and his strut requires a few faster paces to reach where the Roses stand at the end of the reception room, across the fireplace from their hosts. It gives the impression of a child running before they have learned to walk. His eyes are pale grey and protuberant and his fine, fluffy hair, brushed into curls at the front and tied with a green velvet ribbon at the nape, has turned prematurely grey and requires no powder. He has pretensions to nobility and wears a velvet coat of forest green, embroidered in silver, which reeks of sandalwood. He reminds Jean of a frog in human clothing.

His voice is high in pitch, and he enunciates clearly, if a

little too fast to follow. 'Certainly, I met with Eugene Mercier last week, and he showed me the impression. I copied it in a sketch and spoke with my clerk.' There's a pause, and he raises a quizzing glass for emphasis. Jean recognises he is playing with them. He won't be giving anything away without seeking something in return. He gives a little cough before continuing, 'He believes the plain button that was with it to be from our supplier in London, and the other would have been engraved there, in the workshop. We supply the buttons to our piece workers, both in Versailles and here in Paris.' Now, he pauses again to draw a sheet of scented notepaper from his sleeve, flicking it out and holding it at arm's length, to read it.

'Who are your piece workers, and what do they do?' Jacob asks.

A footman is circulating, serving aperitif. Chalonnier stares at the tray. He selects a glass and sips delicately before continuing, 'I have tailors who work for the quality. They make entire suits, or gowns. Each has their own workshop with a team of seamstresses or apprentices. However, some items, such as undergarments are sent to the convents, where either some nuns or the women who seek accommodation with them are paid to make these, or to mend garments.' He explains that clothing is sold on and if it does not fit the new owner, they require fitting to alter the coat, or gown to their measurements. Nothing is wasted, and a coat might have several owners. Jean notices a slightly threadbare ridge on the sleeve of Chalonnier's fine velvet. It too, it appears, is second or third hand.

'You mention convents?' Francine hovers nearby, fanning herself against the heat of the fire- and holding her skirts back to avoid the flames.

Chalonnier nods. The Assembly approved the sale of church property last month, but he tells them that those establishments where children are educated and the sick nursed will remain open. He has several piece workers among the servants to the boarders at Pentemont Abbey- where daughters of the court, including the Royal family and daughters of diplomats such as Thomas Jefferson are among the students. Francine attended a similar school at Passy but knows the regime at Pentemont is very strict.

Jacob wonders how his companions would feel if they suspected there are moves afoot to make the clergy take an oath of loyalty to the Assembly. He's written the date for these amendments into the ledgers himself. He trusts there will be no priests or abbots wishing to follow in the footsteps of Thomas More, willing to die rather than to say a few words.

It all comes down to money, Jacob suspects. The church owns six percent of the land of France, charges everyone a tithe, and while some establishments carry out the word of God, there are younger sons of titled families who hold bishoprics without ever having visited their diocese, choosing instead to pursue a life at court. Some of the plans to elect bishops and make residency in their diocese a condition are surely not so bad if the result is proper reform?

Sandy appears at his wife's elbow, with a glass of aperitif in his hand. He's been listening to Chalonnier but he's been watching Jacob. 'How's your new man Saint Etienne?' he asks. Jean Paul Rabaud Saint Etienne is a Protestant, recently elected as President of the Assembly. Only a few years ago, that would have barred him, along with Necker, from office. 'I hear there's been trouble in Nimes and Toulouse?'

Feelings run high among the good Catholics of the South, Jacob agrees- and it's there, in the areas close to Avignon that the Pope is counting on resistance to the Assembly's decrees. Any sign of Protestant authority might stir up old grudges. He accepts a glass from a tray and sniffs before taking a sip.

'After what those folk did to the Cathars, sending in the Inquisition to torture them, all those years ago, you might find yourself with more trouble than it's all worth,' Sandy suggests.

He has a point. The Pope has influence with the Queen's brother, and Mirabeau and Saint Etienne must tread carefully if a foreign war is likely.

All this time, Chalonnier has been darting glances around the room, obviously looking for potential clients. Jean murmurs apologies and detaches from the conversation to shadow him. There are about thirty at this evening's reception, with a score dining afterwards. Jean, as a mere clerk, will take her meal with the servants. The table in the next room, is set with silver cutlery, gleaming glass and Sevres dishes, and tall wax candles in silver candelabras stand ready to be lit when the doors are fully opened. By a window, keeping away from the fireplace, is the Marquise and her page, Etienne. Chalonnier approaches her, making an elaborate bow and she acknowledges him with a gesture of her closed fan.

They exchange words, and although Jean strains to listen, their voices are lowered and there's a sense of urgency. If Jean is correct, there's been a transfer of information concerning the court. The page, however, is close enough to hear. He keeps his expression passive, as a good servant must- but Jean suspects he would make a useful spy, and intelligence has its own currency, after all.

Chapter 13

Jean hopes to have a word with Etienne at supper, but the Marquise insists on being served at table by her page. Instead, Jean sits at a small table in the butler's pantry with the housekeeper, Margaret, a sensible widow from Aberdeen, whose husband was the Geddes coachman until his death five years ago. They are joined by the secretary, the lady's maid and the valet. The butler, cook and the serving staff dine after the tables upstairs are cleared. At the stairwell through the open door, the scullery maid waits for each course to come down, to whisk the plates away to be cleansed before sauce or gravy congeals. She dined earlier on broth and bread. There's a strict hierarchy in grand houses, that runs from Iceland to Italy. A great deal of money goes into the running of a household, but for the Geddes couple, it is worth every coin. It shows the world 'who we are.' The larger houses at Versailles have twice as many servants, and in the royal palaces, even the King would find it hard to know how many wait at his table or launder his linen.

The pecking order in the household extends to the tableware. The dishes upstairs will be served on fine Sevres and eaten with silver forks, but the servant's hall has glazed stoneware dishes and pewter cutlery

The upper servants have a fine soup to start- the same soup that went up in a tureen for the dining room. Jean savours every mouthful, and the bread that goes with it. The entrée of veal is better than anything she enjoyed at the inn, and the dessert course, of pears preserved in brandy intoxicates with sweetness. Margaret asks about the conversation upstairs and Jean entertains with a description of Chalonnier. The valet takes too big a gulp of his wine and splutters into a napkin.

'Did I speak out of turn?' Jean feels guilty. Sometimes she forgets her strict upbringing in a Calvinist household.

The man smiles and shakes his head. 'Chalonnier is a rogue. Don't let him convince you with his airs and graces- they're all put on. I trained in the same tailor's workshop as him, here in Paris. He's no more an aristocrat than the scullery maid is.' Through the open doorway, the scullery maid, scrubbing a serving platter, looks up and scowls.

He goes on to explain that Chalonnier is an opportunist with a good head for business. 'He took to dealing in second hand clothing, altering to fit the new owner. Everyone knew that if you looked the part, you could enter Versailles and find ways of moving up in the world. He supplied the very dress that Jeanne de la Motte wore to get through the doors. He bought himself noble status to get out of paying his taxes. He's up there touting for business, and the master is encouraging him.'

Jean thinks for a moment, then decides to share what she knows. She relates the story Jacob told her, about finding the body, and going to the Morgue, and the two buttons, describing the engraving. 'I asked Mercier the draper, and he suggested Chalonnier might know more? It seems to be more trouble than it's all worth.'

Women of the Revolution

The table falls silent. Jean looks round to find the page Etienne standing in the doorway. His face is composed- but Jean suspects he has been listening to the discourse. He appears inscrutable, which in a child is a curious thing.

He's been sent to fetch a condiment. Margaret gets up and fetches a small silver dish and hands it to the page. They wait until he is out of earshot before resuming their conversation.

'He tells tales on the servants,' the lady's maid says. 'It wouldn't be the first time one of us got into trouble.'

'He's only a child,' Jean replies.

'A child with the mind of a Machiavelli,' Margaret observes. 'That woman keeps him at her side all the time. Her housekeeper tells me he even sleeps in her private rooms, and Milady sets him to listen in on things that are none of her business. Maybe he thinks she will give him his freedom, but the moment he's not useful to her, she'll have him sent away.'

Perhaps even now, Etienne will be telling Chalonnier of her unkind description?

'You were saying about how Chalonnier built his business?' she prompts the valet.

'It started with second hand coats and gowns,' he continues, 'often sold to those with ideas above their station in life. He developed a skill for tailoring using darts rather than cutting so the pieces could be sold on again and again and had more work than he could feasibly do himself. He took on some apprentices but put it round by word of mouth that he needed piece workers. There are many people with limited means and good needlework skills who are glad of a coin or two in times of need. Chalonnier charges his customers much more than he pays his workers. I altered a coat last month for him, working by candlelight for a week, and he paid me a pittance.'

The lady's maid is nodding. 'The servants of poor women staying in the convents do the fine stitching for him because they need every penny to pay for their bed and board. There's a girl at Pentemont who does nothing but sew on buttons. Perhaps she might be able to help you?'

Jean considers for a moment. Didn't the Chevalier St Georges mention the place? She remembers that Jules told her Lucette was working at the abbey. She resolves to send a message to the girl.

Chapter 14

May, 1790
London

Lewis' New London Tavern and Coffee House has large rooms, thanks to an expansion to accommodate big gatherings. It is seldom empty; the ale is cheap, and it even serves tea and coffee. This makes it the ideal spot; Jacques Rose believes, for his good friend Marat to mingle with others in his situation- temporarily out of favour in France.

He is not surprised to find Suzanne Gregoire and Jeanne de la Motte sitting one evening with a middle-aged artisan who turns out to be their employer.

'Well, if it isn't...'

'Sylvie.' Suzanne snaps- before he can expose her real identity. 'Why Jacques, it is a long time since we met.'

The button maker gets up, gives a half bow and tells Jacques that he won't impose on a gathering of friends. He tidies his coat, sets his hat on his head and scuttles over to have a word with the innkeeper. He casts a glance over his shoulder before he opens the door and leaves.

So, the grand lady Suzanne has taken a job? How the mighty have fallen, Jacques smirks. He hasn't forgiven her for dropping him after the Women's March: leaving him behind like yesterday's laundry. 'I gather you are out of favour in Paris? I heard about your sudden departure.'

'Is that why you and Marat have been skulking around here?' Suzanne does not mince her words. She is fully aware that Marat recently escaped arrest and imprisonment by the skin of his teeth.

'All the best people are in London, these days, haven't you heard? Even Orleans is in town,' he says. Exile suits Jacques, Suzanne thinks. He's grown a couple of inches, and his short, mousy hair no longer looks like it's been hacked off with kitchen shears but is styled to look carelessly windswept. He's smartly dressed too- no loose workman's trousers, but he's found a clean shirt and a jacket that fits his spare frame. He could almost pass for a gentleman.

She's seen rather a lot of gentlemen in the button shop with similarly styled hair, with breeches tucked into highly polished riding boots, and well-cut coats in fine wool showing off brocade waistcoats. These dandies come to collect the engraved silver snuff boxes, that Suzanne had suggested would be an excellent sideline to silver buttons. 'They can be used for snuff of course, but some ladies use such boxes to store the silk patches they use to conceal blemishes on their powdered faces,' she advised, pouting prettily and taking great care to bat her eyelashes at the poor man. Her employer doubled his trade in the month since they arrived. The attractive French lady in the front shop alone is reason for the men to spend their money.

Jeanne, who learned forgery at her father's knee, has a skill at engraving that more than earns their keep. All they must do is to keep their heads down, work hard and save their pennies until their luck changes. The button maker asks questions, and they offer the most evasive of answers.

'As luck will have it,' Jacques tells them, 'We're going back to France soon. It seems we've been missed.'

Discord in the south of France- with the anti-revolutionary riots in Toulouse, Avignon, Vannes and most recently Marseilles have kept the law makers' attention there. The Cordeliers Club has shown there is an appetite for change and rabble rousing. Who better to deliver that than their very own Marat? It is time the People's Friend presses started turning again.

Jacques has not been idle. He's accompanied Marat to meetings, and he's carried out some surveillance on the instructions of Le Maitre, following among others the Duc de Chartres- the man the Girondins see as a potential Constitutional monarch. It's suited King Louis to send his cousin to England in the hope of securing the throne of Brabant. Louis knows it is a waste of time, but he's anxious to keep Philippe from funding civil unrest. Now, it looks as if he is planning to return to France soon too.

Jacques visited the pawnbroker today. Suzanne watched him go in and give a handful of coin to the old woman, who handed him something small in return. She pulls her stool closer to him and under the pretence of whispering a juicy piece of information, she slips a practised hand inside his coat pocket, closing her fingers over what she finds there. She nudges Jeanne's foot to get her attention and passes the item to her below the table.

The women get up, and leave. They wait until they are back in their lodging before they open the little cotton bag to reveal the diamond pin, purloined by Jacques, months ago.

Suzanne checks the stones carefully. Surely had Jacques known they were diamonds; he'd have sold them outright? It seems he's learned the business of biding his time- something she would not have given him credit for a year ago. Perhaps it is time to watch him just a little bit more closely? She's used to having men do her dirty work for her- the group of ruffians that she left behind in Paris were loyal to her, but Jacques is different. His loyalty is to none but himself. In many ways he is just like her.

Chapter 15

Pentemont Abbey occupies the plot at the corner of Rue de Grenelles and Rue de Bellechasse. It's a fine building: extensive work was started by the current abbess, the formidable Marie Catherine Bethisy de Mezieres in 1745. There was fierce competition for the task but the winning design by Pierre Contant d'Ivry, in a blend of rococo and classical styles was only completed seven years ago in 1783. It houses a renowned girls' school, but there's concern that at any moment they might be turned out, and the building handed to the National Guard. The Church is being stripped of its property, and even such an august lady as the abbess, is not exempt.

Jean the clerk is on a mission. The abbey has sets of rooms, occupied by ladies of good standing in need of rest- which translates as women seeking separation from their spouses. One such lady is the estranged wife of Alexandre Beauharnais. Marie Joseph Rose Tascher de la Pagerie has her daughter Hortense and son, Eugene with her in her apartment. She's allowed to come and go as she pleases but must spend her evenings in the Abbey. This is no punishment, because the salons in the building often host lively entertainments and debates. Francine talks of the writers and musicians she has met on the evenings when she visits with her sister and the Marquise.

The countess Beauharnais, aunt to the absent husband, and godmother to Hortense is a playwright and friend of Olympe de Gouges.

Beauharnais, according to Mirabeau, is a bad lot, who prefers the company of mistresses and the women of the Paris brothels. 'He was due to marry the middle de Pagerie girl, but she died and the youngest girl was too young. Poor Marie Josephe Rose, the oldest of the three sisters, drew the short straw. He certainly didn't love her- but he could only inherit if he took a wife. Her parents were relieved they got a daughter wed without a dowry, and they packed her off to France and washed their hands of her.'

Jacob tells Jean that Beauharnais was one of the first nobles to throw his lot in with the Third Estate. 'He's passionate about the Revolution, and he's likely to hold high office soon.'

However, Jean's business is with the women of Madame Beauharnais' household, and one of these is Lucette, daughter of Mercier's coachman. Jean sent a letter and received a reply, instructing her to go to a side door on the Rue de Grenelles at two o'clock. Jean makes a point of being there a quarter of an hour early, and paces up and down the pavement, until she hears a smoothly oiled bolt drawn back.

Anyone with mischief on their mind would assume the pretty maid, in her pale grey starched cotton dress and spotless white apron, is meeting the young clerk for an assignation. She looks up and down the street, to check they are unobserved, then ushers Jean into the narrow staircase that leads up to the Beauharnais apartment, and carefully bolts the door again.

WOMEN OF THE REVOLUTION

Lucette is a servant who assists Madame Beauharnais' lady's maid. As recently as a year ago, she'd dreamed of working at Versailles, and her current situation suits her aspirations. Jean knows she's the child of the court musician Gianfranco Valenti and his wife, Ottilie- once a favourite of Marie Antoinette. Jean saw Ottilie in Charenton asylum, nursing a doll she took for her lost daughter. Jacob Rose tells Jean that he will reunite Lucette with her birth parents, but that must be at a time when the girl will be able to cope with the truth. Lucette still believes the cook and the coachman- formerly the innkeeper and the cook of the inn where Jacob dined- to be her birth family. Furthermore, the shock of seeing a grown-up Lucette could do a great deal of damage to Ottilie, who has taken years to find peace.

They climb one flight of stairs to a small landing with several doors leading to the Beauharnais apartment, and Jean gets a glimpse of pale blue walls adorned with mirrors and paintings. This is no ascetic cell, but a comfortable, well-furnished room. The bills are paid by Alexandre – but his wife's tastes are lavish. There is a huge arrangement of fresh cut roses in a vase on a spindly legged table, and beside it a dish of marron glaces. Jean's mouth waters at the sight of the sweets- they are a favourite that she only rarely enjoys.

The maids' apartments are in the attics, three floors above. The small room that Lucette ushers Jean into is whitewashed and smells of lavender and starch. A tiny stove bears a kettle, bubbling to a rolling boil. An older woman, dressed in dark blue, with a cap covering her hair, is pressing a linen petticoat with a flat iron. She straightens up when Lucette introduces the clerk and offers a seat by the window. Jean sits on the window bench and twists her body to look through the panes at the street below. To Jean's right there's a large basket, piled with garments waiting to be pressed.

Lucette introduces the older woman as Marie Lannoy,

personal maid to Madame Beauharnais.

'Thank you for coming to see us, sir,' Marie begins, 'but to what do we owe this visit?'

'Your name, Madame, was on a list of those who work for the tailor Chalonnier. I'm looking for the person who sewed an engraved silver button on to a pair of breeches at the start of this year. He tells my employer that piece work, such as this, is done in this abbey. Are you able to help us?'

Marie indicates the basket. 'I receive this sort of work from Chalonnier, and distribute it to other maids. Our employers might be extravagant when it comes to themselves, but they often forget to pay our wages, and we do a little sewing or mending to give us something to save for our own needs. There's nothing wrong with that, is there?'

Jean notices that the maid is slender, and looks tired, but her face is kind. 'I alter gowns and launder and mend garments. I leave the sewing on of buttons to Lucette here.'

Jean hands over a sheet of paper on which she has sketched the engraving from the wax impression of the button. 'Do either of you remember seeing a silver button with this motif among your work?'

'Might I ask why a button is of such importance?' Marie asks, turning the paper over in her hands. There's a burn mark on her right hand, and her nails, which are manicured, are short and tidy and buffed to a shine.

'The owner of the breeches was pulled out of the Seine, and is in the Paris Morgue, waiting to be claimed for burial,' Jean replies.

Marie's pale face grows even whiter, and she collapses onto a chair beside the fireplace. Lucette, with great presence of mind, grabs the iron and places it on the hot plate of the stove.

'I think a drink of water?' Jean murmurs. Lucette pours

from an earthenware jug into a plain glass, and hands it to Marie.

'This did not come from Chalonnier. The owner and his wife are friends of Madame. They left some mending to be done. We do not get paid for that. He lost one of the engraved buttons and we needed to send to Mercier for a plain replacement.'

'Can you tell us his name, Madame? We can contact the family if we know who they are and where we can find them?'

Marie sips at her water. Her hand is shaking, and Jean wonders if she is in shock. 'Virginie de la Croix. She's a friend of Madame, from her childhood in the islands. She's married to- was married to Antoine Deschamps. He was like a brother to my lady when they were growing up.'

'Where can she be found?' Jean asks carefully.

Chapter 16

Marie Grosholz has the death mask ready. It is placed on a side table and covered with a silk cloth. The body, embalmed, is in the cold room below, and it will be less of a shock to the grieving widow to make the identification in this way. The mortuary is cool and she is glad of the warmth of the smock over her dress.

Present at the identification is Virginie with her friend Madame Beauharnais, along with Jacob Rose and Curtius. Virginie is as dowdy and plain as her friend Rose, as Marie Joseph Rose Beauharnais prefers to be called, is beautiful. The latter is slender and has chestnut hair and hazel eyes that look almost gold in the bright morning sunshine outside the Morgue. She treats her friend with great tenderness, placing an arm round the shorter woman, and offering a handkerchief to dry tears. Her voice is low pitched and has a musical quality which Jacob finds intriguing.

Virginie is dry eyed and appears to be more in control than Jacob might have suspected. Curtius greets them at the door, and ushers them inside.

Jacob gently explains how and where the body was found

and how it came to be at the Morgue. 'We had no report of a missing person matching his description. You were unaware your husband was absent?'

Marie Grosholz offers a seat to the visitors, and Virginie sits down, smoothing her wide, out of fashion, skirts. Rose chooses to remain standing.

The mask, still draped in its silk cover, is carefully lifted to the table in front of Virginie and uncovered. Marie Grosholz stands back, hands clasped before her. Jacob looks at the image and is struck by how true a likeness it is. He might be staring at the face of the man he saw pulled from the river.

'Is this your husband?' Curtius asks, gently.

The woman looks as if she also has been turned to a wax likeness. She nods, but says, 'I do not understand. The last time I saw him, at the end of January he was on board a ship bound for England. He had business in Manchester and was then going back to the islands. How could he have fallen into the Seine?'

Curtius confers with his niece, and they ask if Madame Deschamps could bear to view the embalmed corpse, and to look at his clothing. They must have a confirmation that this is indeed her husband before the body can be released for burial.

She shakes her head, but Rose says, 'I knew Antoine well. He was a childhood friend. I will view the body, but perhaps Virginie might look at the clothing? I am told that some mending was done by my maid. She is waiting outside.'

Marie is sent to fetch the maid, and Curtius escorts Rose downstairs to view the embalmed corpse. Jacob hears her light footsteps follow the heavier ones of Curtius, as she descends to the Hades below.

The maid, Marie Lannoy, is known to Jacob through his clerk, who tells him she takes good care of her mistress, and of their young friend Lucette. She is a soberly dressed woman, with a shawl drawn over her plain blue gown and a frilled cap covering what looks like light brown hair. Marie Grosholz brings the set of garments to the table, removing the death mask to the side counter. Marie Lannoy lifts each garment in turn, shows it to the widow, who examines each item closely. Jacob suspects the woman needs spectacles as she needs to hold the buttons up to her nose to scrutinise the pattern.

'These are the breeches that we mended. I recognise the buttons,' the maid says.

Virginie remains as if turned to stone. She passes a hand over the breeches, but at the sight of the slashed shirt, she turns her head away.

Marie Grosholz has seen many grieving widows, but she does not see pain or loss in this woman's face. Rather, she sees a mask of a different sort. This widow knows more about this death than she is prepared to show the world.

In contrast, Rose emerges from the basement, holding a handkerchief to her eyes. She embraces Virginie, and says, 'There is no doubt, my dear. It is Antoine.'

CHAPTER 17

1ˢᵗ June, 1790

Jacob is invited to take supper with Sandy Geddes and looks forward to an enlightening evening. This time, Francine is absent, visiting her sister's house at Versailles, and the small gathering consists of Geddes, two Scottish merchants whom Jacob has known since his studies at the Scots College, and writer Guillaume Thomas Francois Raynal.

The dinner is heavier this evening, but the dishes are those enjoyed by Scotsmen. A rich broth is followed by a casserole of lamb, with carrots in red wine, and the pudding is Atholl brose, a particular favourite of Sandy's and of their guest of honour. The dishes are set out on the sideboard, and they are helping themselves to the food. This gives the serving staff less work, but it's also to allow them to talk freely without fear of betrayal of their guest of honour.

Jacob knows that Raynal, a former priest, has written extensively and controversially about the Caribbean islands, and he needs his advice. Raynal was only allowed to return from exile on the condition that he remained outside of

Paris, and the reason why this evening's gathering is small, is to protect the elderly man from arrest. This is a friend and collaborator of Diderot. Raynal is a member of the Royal Society of Great Britain but to many in France he represents a threat to public safety.

The identification of the dead man pulled from the river as Antoine Deschamps has entailed correspondence with Jacob's cousin, George Rose. There's concern about how a man last seen aboard a ship bound for England, and later the West Indies, was pulled out of the Seine less than a fortnight later. That wretched silver button has not only proved a clue but led to the opening of a dish of worms.

When Jacob named the dead man and sent Jean's drawing of the button design to George, he didn't anticipate the complexity of the response.

The button was engraved with a tree, with a recumbent hound at its base. The button maker, a man whose business has recently boomed with the advent of a new engraver and sales clerk, looked out the records kept by his late mother. The design was for the Half Moon Plantations on Martinique, St Lucia and Saint Domingue on Hispaniola, owned by the late Camille Deschamps- a man who owned much property in the islands. 'We produced the buttons in silver for the family members and in pewter for the livery of household servants,' he told George's clerk. 'The Deschamps family were among our most valued customers.'

George wrote: 'As you know, there have been times when the island of Saint Lucia has changed hands between Great Britain and France, and we have found it prudent to have intelligence from paid officials across the islands of the Caribbean. Old Deschamps was not perhaps the sort of man we should have recruited under normal circumstances. He had a wife in France and a son, estranged for many years but he also had numerous offspring from liaisons with coloured or mulatto former slaves, who he trusted to run the plantations. Your missing man turns out to be the son of a plantation manager on Hispaniola. He's a grandson of Camille, and we had him on our list of agents. He was educated in Martinique, at a boarding school, and was a friend of some of the prominent families. His reports mentioned uprisings among the enslaved workers in Saint Domingue, of late.'

Jacob thought that made perfect sense. The woman, Rose Beauharnais, displayed a greater fondness for her childhood friend than his own wife- whose reaction still perplexes him.

Sandy Geddes falls silent at the table. He pours himself a glass of port and sips it before speaking. 'Deschamps, you say?'

'Antoine Deschamps, yes.' Jacob turns to his friend.

'I might be wrong, but I have the bill of sale for a house slave- that wee lad Etienne that is in the Marquise' household. Andrew Cargill made a fuss about the fact he was sold by his own half-brother. I couldn't swear to it, but I think the name of the seller was Deschamps.'

'Could you look out the documents, please?' Jacob asks. The evening is warm, but an icy chill has worked its way down his spine.

'They're in my warehouse. It will be next week before I can lay hands on them,' the merchant replies.

Raynal is toying with oatcakes and a hunk of farmhouse cheese on the plate before him, He helps himself to grapes and lifts a morsel to his mouth.

'A bad business when a brother sells his own kin,' he says. 'Sooner or later, justice will be done. I've said it before and will say it again, that in the colonies when the negroes finally have a chief to lead them into battle, they will seek vengeance.'

One of the merchants turns and says, 'Perhaps they already have such a leader- and he's started his work right here in Paris.'

Sandy pours more port into Jacob's glass and says, 'Is it prudent to become embroiled in these affairs? You've enough on your plate with the business of the Assembly. Just leave it to the police?'

Jacob shrugs. 'They've already decided it was a duel gone wrong and a wounded man fell into the river and drowned. As far as they're concerned, the case is closed. The surgeon who did the postmortem found a ligature mark, and no water in the stomach, which suggested he was dead before he was put into the river. No, my interest is due to the fact the dead man was a known agent of the British government. George wants to know who wanted him dead. I want to know if he shared anything that affects my role.'

Jacob gives Sandy a thin smile. 'Perhaps now you understand why I was reluctant to work for the Assembly? It is impossible to serve two masters.'

CHAPTER 18

It is good to be back in Paris, Jacques thinks, lifting his face to the summer sunshine, as he leaves the print shop. He enjoyed living incognito in London for a while, but he ran into some fellows from Aberdeen, who called him by his real name rather too loudly for comfort. Johnnie Rose is still on a list of those wanted for sedition, and he really doesn't fancy a long voyage to the Antipodean colonies. Best to leave that for the martyrs.

Fortunately, Marat decided that Paris needed The People's Friend- the Revolution is moving swiftly into a new phase. The power of the Church has been stopped by the Assignat, and now there's a move to remove the titles, powers and privileges of the nobility. Scotland could learn a lot from the Parisians, Jacques thinks.

They're living in the Cordeliers quarter, close to the convent which is one of the early Church casualties. The group that meets in the cloisters is energetic in its desire for universal male suffrage and direct democracy- exactly the sort of thing that his fellows in Aberdeen had been after. They've taken an open eye as their symbol and their motto:

liberty, equality and fraternity can stir even the hardest heart. It is their job, Desmoulins reminds them, to scrutinise the actions of the Assembly and to ensure they don't backslide.

Most of the gang are from the educated middle-class bourgeoisie- women as well as men, but there are some right ragged rabble rousers as well. It helps too, that they are close neighbours with the men of the moment- Robespierre, Danton and Desmoulins. As a printer, Jacques also helps with Desmoulins' History of the Revolutions of France and Brabant, a regular publication which is anti-royalist and pro revolutionary. Desmoulins has a speech impediment which only vanishes when his dander is up and has no effect on his eloquence in print.

Things are moving swiftly and new alliances are created daily. Sometimes Jacques can barely keep up. Gone are the days when Desmoulins and Le Maitre were working with the Duke of Orleans and Mirabeau. This new crowd are talking about republicanism. If it works for the Americans, then surely it can work here in France?

Marat was right about letting Suzanne Gregoire have her little brooch back. Jacques rather enjoyed having her pick his pocket in that inn. Mirabeau has put it about that they've done a deal with Nicholas de la Motte and that the diamonds are now the property of the Assembly – it means if she tries to show her sneaky little face back in France that she can be arrested for theft. He hopes he'll be there to see her dragged off to jail. In the meantime, he's left a little note for her employer, who might be interested in her past misdemeanours and those of his engraver.

He's still adept at theft himself. The other day he watched his twin leave Jacob's premises, satchel over shoulder, and took the opportunity to let himself in. The skeleton key still works easily on the locks, and he spent a leisurely hour or two, reading the documents they keep in the desk. There wasn't much of interest. The practice must be just ticking over, and Jacob can't be bringing work home? The thought struck him that there might be another desk and he let himself into the man's bedchamber.

The cabinet in the alcove is new. He hadn't noticed that in his previous incursions. He ran his fingers over the polished dark wood. There were small drawers which yielded folded stockings and a bag of coins. He found a small piece of sealing wax with the impression of a tree and a dog, which he pocketed. Nothing to interest him. He climbed to his twin's attic, and rummaged in the box she keeps below the bed, looking for the family seal, but it looked as if she keeps that on her person these days. Her narrow bed was neatly made, and there was a book on her night-stand. A Bible? It turned out to be a novel by Daniel Defoe. These June evenings offer enough daylight to read in the attic. Typical of Jeannie, whose love for books he didn't share- unless they were about politics.

It is a neat little house. The plain walls and window shutters are reminiscent of a monastic cell. Only a small looking glass or framed sketch as decoration in the upper chambers and a chiming clock in the business room. He opened the door in the corner and descended the staircase to the scullery. He noted the copper pans, each in their place, and the small stack of plates and cups, and the silverware- just enough for the needs of a small household. He sought out the tin box and opened it knowing it would contain shortbread. Snapping a biscuit in half it looked to be a fresh supply. He put the biscuit in his mouth and chewed thoughtfully. This is the life that might have been his: the work of a notary's clerk, living under his employer's roof, visiting his sister, who by rights should have been a lady's companion- work suited to the spinster he always thought her to be.

Julie MP Adams

He left the desk unlocked to let her know he's back. He slipped out and was in the narrow street only moments before her return. He slipped into a doorway and watched her open the gate, close it behind her, and let herself in. He smiled as he thought of her finding the signs he had been there.

Now, as he accepts a glass of red wine from a buxom woman with a hard face, he digs in his pocket for coin, and his fingers close over the piece of sealing wax. Why would Jacob Rose keep a used seal? He will ask Marat when he arrives.

CHAPTER 19

29th June, 1790

Versailles is a ghost palace. The beauty remains, but as a ghost of its former grandeur. Gone are the days of the Sun King and his successor. The workmen in the gardens continue to prune and mow, and to plant the borders. Their wages are paid, but there is no longer a king or queen giving approval. The monarch and his consort live quietly at the Tuileries, with a smaller court. It is a dull place, and there's an underlying tinge of fear. They are guarded by Lafayette and his men, who prevent the mob from entering to cause harm- but also prevent the King and Queen from trying to leave. They are prisoners in their own palace.

The nobles lose their titles after the Assembly passes laws to remove aristocratic privilege on the nineteenth of June. Some of them, like Beauharnais, already joined the Third Estate to obtain power in the new regime. After all, the King seldom allowed anyone other than himself and his small group of ministers to hold any real political power: revolution has offered opportunities to make a difference.

Others actively plan a counter revolution. The Marquise' and her husband belong to this movement. She already has a growing reputation as the hostess of a salon, and while she will invite revolutionaries, in the hope of picking their brains, if there's no hope of turning their loyalty, she courts those Versailles residents who face either a life without titles, leaving the town for their country estates, or those who may join the ever-growing numbers of emigres.

Tonight, she hosts a musical evening. Some of those musicians left behind in the palace seek work and hire themselves out as string quartets and smaller orchestras.

Guiseppe Valenti and his son, Gianfranco lead tonight's entertainments in a programme of Mozart string quartets. The audience who come for the music sit on spindly chairs, fanning themselves against the heat of the evening and the candelabra flames. Others, circulate in the ante rooms, holding quiet conversations in corners, under the pretext of seeking a drink or an ice.

Francine, on a visit to her sister, enjoys the music, but has a stomach cramp which can only be eased by movement. She hears her hostess and her own sister talking quietly, and she slips behind a pillar to listen.

'They met in Lower Silesia. A place called Reichenbach. The English diplomats were there, along with those of the Emperor and the Prussians and the United Provinces.' The Marquise can barely contain her excitement. Her eyes glitter, and not for the first time, she reminds Francine of a fox near chickens.

'What do you think will come of it?' her sister asks.

'The Queen wants her brother to send troops,' the Marquise whispers, 'and the English would dearly love to punish Lafayette for helping the Americans. Who knows? It might mean war.'

Francine's brother, an officer who served with Lafayette,

died at the Battle of Rhode Island. Their father died soon afterwards of a broken heart. War means more deaths. The prospect fills her with dismay. Her mother was left with two daughters to marry off and no money.

She hears her name called. Her sister has spotted her, and the conversation has turned to the music.

'Isn't that the violinist from the Women's March?' her sister asks.

The Marquise flicks her fan open and uses it vigorously for several moments. 'It appears that he was a prisoner of the Bastille, held on his release by some of the revolutionaries. He found his way into the palace and turned out to be the son of old Valenti.'

'Wasn't he the one who ran off with Ottilie?' Francine's sister asks.

Francine excuses herself and returns to her seat. The quartet is almost over. The violinist's eyes are on the sheet music on the stand, but there's a sadness in them that makes Francine's heart ache for him. She knows the woman he loved and married is in a cell in Charenton asylum, and that their daughter, raised by servants is a maid, somewhere in Paris. That much she has gleaned from listening to Sandy and Jacob. She's a poor intelligence officer, but she's sure they will be interested in what she has just heard. The company of her sister and her society friends has less appeal for Francine. She will cut her visit short and return to Paris tomorrow.

From the corner of her eye, she sees the page, Etienne. He too is tucked behind a pillar. The silver tray in his hand is empty and he holds it down at his side. His expression is impassive, but she wonders how much he hears, and if the Marquise is aware there might be a spy under her roof? Might he in fact be spying on the guests?

Chapter 20

4th July, 1790

Cargill's ship docks at Le Havre and he arrives at the Geddes house bringing a chest of goods that delight Sandy: bottles of malt whisky from the Isle of Skye, and even a bottle of the liqueur made from whisky and honey to the Bonnie's Prince's recipe. There are the latest English novels, some books of poetry by Robert Burns and a length of fine wool cloth that will make a handsome coat. He brings correspondence from Edinburgh and from London and copies of the Edinburgh and London newspapers. Francine orders a special supper and has his usual room prepared. The sea captain is with them for a week while the French part of his cargo is loaded for the onward voyage.

As always, Sandy sends for Jacob and Jean – these visits offer useful information and opportunities to send those documents which cannot travel by the normal posts. The captain will drop these with a trusted courier in the Channel Islands on his way to Hispaniola.

The evening is warm and they dine early and take their

glasses of brandy out to the enclosed garden, where they can talk without fear of being overheard. As the light fades, fireflies dance round the flower beds, and the scent of lavender and roses fills the air. A fountain plays in the centre of the beautifully tended space.

Francine tells Jacob what she overheard at the Marquise' soiree. 'Is she right? Will there be war?'

Andrew Cargill shrugs his shoulders. 'I don't know about war, but His Majesty's Navy is press ganging men from the ports. I've lost too many of my crews. I don't let them near taverns when they go ashore.'

Jacob is thoughtful and lifts his glass to examine the inch of golden liquid remaining. 'I had intelligence of the Silesian conference from my cousin. I doubt the British Treasury can afford another war, but it appears this is the result of an appeal from Louis to his wife's kin, and they don't want to proceed without the support of other countries.'

Sandy approaches a rose bush and pulls a bloom towards him, swearing as a thorn pricks his finger. He thrusts the digit into his glass- alcohol is a cure all- then sucks the finger. 'There are spies everywhere, these days. Who do you think told the Marquise about the meeting?'

Francine's attention is taken by a firefly, and she bends to try to capture it in her fingers. 'She has people all over the place – those soirees of hers are an excuse. Have you noticed that she seems to depend on that little page- the one you brought last year. Etienne? Jean here tells me he listens at doors.'

Sandy observes 'I told you last week that we brought him over? I found the paperwork for the transaction. He was listed on the manifest as S Field. Stephen Field?'

The sky is darkening. Jean notices the look on Andrew Cargill's face – his jaw is clenched, and his hands are thrust into his pockets.

Jacob remembers something. 'That dead man in the Morgue- Deschamps- was thought to be a British spy. George wasn't too sure about him, though. Seems there's some stirrings of trouble in the islands. Did you see anything of note on your last voyage, Cargill?'

'When we put into harbour yesterday, there was a ship just in from Martinique. It seems there's an uprising there. The enslaved folk had high hopes the Assembly would free them- but it seems they're worse off than before.' Cargill sighs.

He takes three paces and turns, hands still in his pockets. 'Deschamps, did you say? That's Field in French isn't it?'

Jacob nods.

'I picked up a Deschamps from Le Havre back in January and dropped him off when we made harbour in Folkestone on my way back to Scotland. I thought there was something familiar about the name at the time, but I couldn't quite say what. I'm wondering now if he wasn't the one who sold the wee lad last year?'

'You are sure you collected him? He was pulled out of the Seine less than a fortnight later.'

'Aye, I'm sure. I watched him walk down the gangplank. I certainly didn't take him back to France and kill him if that's what you're asking, Jacob Rose.' His voice sounds shrill. Jean wonders if he's telling the truth.

Someone wanted Antoine Deschamps dead. Cargill's distaste for the man is obvious, but he's not a murderer. Whoever killed the man did not act alone, Jacob suspects. Perhaps he needs to find out more about what Antoine Deschamps was doing?

Chapter 21

All other plans are set aside for the huge Festival of the Federation on the Fourteenth of July, 1790. Deputies from all over France are gathered for this event on the Champ de Mars outside the city. Huge earthworks have been raised on all four sides where folk can sit and get a better view of the proceedings. Volunteers worked for weeks with wheelbarrows to construct these, and a new song, Ah Ca Ira, was their refrain. A temporary bridge of boats was assembled to allow the participants to cross the Seine to the venue.

The King and the Royal Family, heads of what the Constituent Assembly now regards as a Constitutional Monarchy occupy a tent at one end, directly opposite the triumphal archway, through which the National Guard march. In the middle is an altar on which a special mass will be said by the Bishop of Autun, Charles Talleyrand. This will be an opportunity for the King to also swear an oath of fealty to the constitution- even though it will be at least a year before it is fully ratified. As Jacob knows all too well, a lot can happen in a year.

There are representatives of the new United States of

Julie MP Adams

America- and their banner of stars and stripes flies proudly over the seats where John Paul Jones sits beside Thomas Paine. It is the first time the flag has been unfurled outside their own territories. The British observers, in contrast, are keeping a low profile.

Jacob, as Usher, is seated halfway up one of the mounds, beside a deputy from Lyon and his younger wife, who is introduced as Madame Roland, ('call me Manon'). She's a woman Jacob would not automatically think of as beautiful, but a fierce intelligence emanates from her, which reminds him of Olympe de Gouges. She has an oval face, with large grey eyes and abundant light brown hair.

She's delighted with this event. 'What better than to see that we have a Constitutional Monarchy where everybody plays their part,' she declaims. He rather enjoys their conversation- she quotes Jean Jacques Rousseau, is familiar with recent events- and thoroughly agrees with having the clergy take an oath of loyalty. Of course, Lyons is in the part of the country, where the Pope has a great deal of influence. There have been recent riots in support of the clergy, which, she says, have cost her and her husband many sleepless nights.

'In the past, it was the nobles who settled disputes, and so far there's nothing in place to deal with crimes. Do you know if they will appoint anyone to run courts? I've even heard of lawlessness in the streets of Paris!'

He tells her there are plans to appoint justices of the peace- 'Rather like the local courts in England,' but advises her to keep that information to herself for the time being.

She is keen to know who everyone is, and he points out the Marquise and her husband, sitting two rows below them, and Mirabeau, seated close to the King. His friend is not looking at all well. He has had too many crises to deal with, not least of which included that meeting at Reichenbach, which some of the Assembly now believe was the result of an approach by the Queen and the King's younger brother, Artois. He's spoken to Jacob already about changing his will. If Mirabeau is gone, there's nobody who can hold everyone and everything together. The factions within the Assembly could undo all the good work.

When the time comes for the Royal oath, Louis is now known not as King of France and Navarre but King of the French. He repeats the words automatically, without real emotion, and Marie Antoinette, holding the hand of her son, says 'This is my son, who like me, joins in the same sentiments.'

Jacob thinks they both wish they were anywhere but here, on this day.

Manon Roland tells him she is looking forward to the feast later in the day, at Chateau de la Muette. Twenty thousand people are invited to this great event, which will be the biggest party ever held outside Versailles, she tells him. Her eyes are shining. Jacob only hopes that history will prove her right- and him wrong.

This day has been engineered; he knows all too well. Too many things lie in the way of achieving a peaceful state. There are rumours that the Pope is deeply unhappy with proposals for the Civil Constitution of the clergy. Furthermore, the people of Avignon- territory the pontiff has always considered part of the papal states, have asked to become officially part of France. Jacob knows that the Assembly are delaying their response, out of concern it may lead to war. He doesn't think he will enjoy the four days of feasting ahead, one little bit.

Chapter 22

August 1st, 1790
London

'I have three snuff boxes ready for engraving,' the button maker tells Jeanne, 'And the customer will call this evening to collect them.' He has a dilemma. His trade has increased, and there is no doubt that is largely down to his two assistants. One is an adept engraver; the other is an excellent salesperson. However, he's worried over a slip of paper- a poison pen letter, which implies the ladies are far from honest, and that one of them is a convicted felon. It gives their real names and accuses them of using an alias- something that no law-abiding woman would do, surely?

In Cheapside, most people have something to hide, including him. However, he's also had visits from people he knows to be government men, who are taking an unhealthy interest in his customers as well as his staff.

There's the business of the button engravings too. His mother produced the original sketches for old Camille Deschamps when he was a small child. He remembers the

Women of the Revolution

Frenchman visiting as he played with a toy horse under the counter. There was a whiff of spices and sugar, and a voice he can recall as musical in its intonation. The visitor bent down to ruffle his hair and ask the name of the toy horse.

He replied the horse was called Bucephalus- the name from his father's stories of Alexander the Great. Father was educated and knew Latin and Greek- which helped his mother with the crests and designs for their wealthy customers.

'Ah, the horse's master wept for the lack of new worlds to conquer,' the Frenchman said. He told him about his lands in Hispaniola, St Lucia and Martinique, islands that the child could only imagine.

They made the first set of buttons and on the next visit the Frenchman declared his delight and placed an order so big, Mother could take no other work on for two months. Every few years, another order would be placed, using the pattern in her record book, but this time the supply would be collected by a sea captain, who would deliver them to the islands. The Frenchman never returned.

He told this to a government clerk, who wrote down everything he said. The man waited until his engraver and assistant had left on an errand, to come into the shop. He asked why there was such interest in a simple button, and the man said it was of some importance, but could not divulge who needed the information. He's not seen him since.

Now, after a decade, there's a repeat order for those buttons. He's to have them ready by the end of the month. He watches Jeanne at her table, the tools of her trade laid out neatly, squinting at the design she is tracing on the snuff boxes. He might be watching his mother- but this one holds her secrets close to her and if he tries to draw her out, a shutter comes down.

He wonders what his staff and this order have to do with

what is happening across the Channel in France? His friend in the tavern, who likes to know what's going on in the world, gets the foreign newspapers. He's particularly fond of the People's Friend- after all, its editor and writer, Marat was staying nearby for some months this year after he fell out with the Assembly. It seems Marat has called for five hundred aristocrats to be executed to save the Revolution. The button maker isn't too fond of the British aristocracy, but without them, his business wouldn't last very long, even if they do take ages to pay their bills.

It's always interesting to hear the news from other countries. It seems that there's been fire raising in Paris. Londoners have 1666 engraved on their hearts- and nobody goes to bed in Cheapside without checking the fireplace is doused for the night.

He heats up silver in the retort, ready to pour into the button moulds. Work will keep him busy and steady his mind for a while. He will think about the women tomorrow.

CHAPTER 23

The Palais Royal, originally the palace of the great Cardinal Richelieu, is situated opposite the Louvre, and thanks to the generosity of the Duke of Orleans, the gardens and covered galleries are a popular meeting place for all and sundry.

Jacques has an appointment to meet Le Maitre here. He doesn't trust him, but he knows he's in with the faction in favour of a Constitutional Monarchy- but the king they have in mind is certainly not Louis. He's known Le Maitre for over a year, but the man has never revealed his real identity, other than to a handful of agents, including, Jacques suspects, Suzanne Gregoire.

The man flits in and out of print shops where Jacques works, including those of Marat and of Desmoulins, as well as the larger papers. He's a source of intelligence, which they are grateful for, which is why Jacques has been ordered to smarten himself up and blend in.

Those long galleries with pillars are much loved by ladies, who drift along in pairs, skirts taking up most of the space. At least they no longer wear those ridiculous panniers where the skirts are two yards wide- the milkmaid fashion of narrower garments allows two to walk abreast. Jacques is impatient and dodges into the open where almost immediately he bumps into a clerk, document bag slung across his shoulder, who keeps his head down.

'Not so fast,' he says, grabbing the clerk by the shoulder. 'Not even a word for your own brother?'

Jean darts a look of pure poison at him and tries to wriggle from his grasp.

'Not even for a bit of information your employer would like to have?' She shrugs herself free, straightens her back and looks him full in the face.

He produces the scrap of wax from his pocket. 'I wondered why Jacob was keeping this, and then I reckoned it was an impression- some sort of seal?'

'You've no right to go into our house,' she retorts.

'You've made drawings of that seal and shown them around,' he says, calmly. 'Something to do with a dead man? Crested buttons?'

She nods. She should have known that sooner or later her twin would get wind of their investigation.

'Buttons ordered from a workshop in Gutter Lane in London? The same workshop where Suzanne Gregoire is working alongside Jeanne de la Motte?'

The look on her face tells him he's had the desired effect. She'll be upset, now and she will run straight to Jacob with that information. He knows that Jacob will pass it on. Now all he needs to do is wait. It's high time Suzanne got her comeuppance. Jacques was happy enough to be seduced when he was younger, but now he sees her for what she is- manipulative and devious and allied to enemies of the Revolution. He's being a good citizen, passing on information through his twin to the Usher. It doesn't hurt to do the occasional good deed- especially when it will do someone else an ill turn.

Chapter 24

10th September 1790
Paris

Jean is delighted to receive an invitation to lunch at the Mercier house and accepts happily, especially when she discovers the cousin is staying on another visit. Mercier has some news for her also, which he wishes to impart in person.

The city of Nancy, the eastern capital of France, where the cousin hoped to stay with family, has been the site of a mutiny in the French army, on a scale unheard of before. 'My poor nephew was caught up in it,' the woman wails to Jean.

Of course, Jean knows there has been dissent in the regular army for years- long before the Revolution. The officers are staunchly Royalist, but the men have drifted towards Jacobin membership, and until the requirement for officers to be from the nobility was recently abolished, the non-commissioned officers were firmly on the side of the men. Giles, the nephew, had planned to apply to the regular army for a commission but had changed his mind and joined

Julie MP Adams

Lafayette's National Guard.

At the end of August, three regiments were stationed in Nancy: the King's regiment, the Swiss mercenaries and the cavalry. The men demanded to see the accounts, confined the officers to their barracks and took charge of the pay chests. 'They claimed they hadn't been paid and that the officers had been less than honest.'

'The Swiss officers overcame their mutineers and they used a terrible punishment against the ringleaders. They made them run the gauntlet.'

Jean could imagine the torture of running between two lines of men, each with a flail or weapon used on the victim.

However, this only made the mutineers even more determined, and Jean knows from Jacob, that the National Constituent Assembly ordered General Bouille to march from Metz to Nancy with a company of four and a half thousand regular soldiers backed up by the National Guard. Giles was among the National Guardsmen.

'They ordered the mutineers to release their officers and hand over some of the ringleaders,' the cousin tells Jean. 'It looked as if they were going to do so, until...' She lifts a lace edged handkerchief to her eyes, and Jean offers a drink of water, which she accepts, and sips, before continuing. 'Just in front of the Stainville Gate, dedicated to those who died in the American wars, some of the mutineers wheeled out a loaded canon. That poor young man, Andre Desilles, one of the junior officers, stood in front of it and tried to talk them out of firing it.'

Desilles was shot down, and the cannon was fired into the loyal troops. Sixty of them died, and Bouille gave the order to charge. The fighting raged for three hours and over five hundred people died- civilians as well as soldiers.

'That's why I've come back,' the cousin sobs. 'My sister's house was in the same street. It's in ruins now.'

Women of the Revolution

Jean offers her condolences, but it transpires that the sister and brother-in-law have business in Paris and their accommodation has no space for Mercier's cousin. Several of their servants perished in the fighting- one of them simply trying to ascertain what was happening on their doorstep. The repairs on the house will take months at the very least.

Mercier observes, 'Those Swiss officers are ruthless. The ringleaders will be broken on the wheel or hanged.' He crosses himself. 'They might have brought it upon themselves, but a mutiny suggests nobody can be trusted.'

They are drinking coffee after lunch, when Jean asks Mercier what was so important, he needed to tell her in person?

'Madame Deschamps visited our shop at Versailles last week. For the first time this year, she paid her bill in full, and asked for the goods she ordered to be sent to the house of a certain Marquise?'

'A Marquise who has a page boy from Hispaniola?'

He nods and helps himself to one of his cousin's excellent dainty little cakes.

'The Marquise' family name, of course, is Deschamps. It seems there's a matter concerning a Will? And while it is being settled, they've seen fit to offer hospitality to the grieving widow. She's been sponging off Madame Beauharnais, but it seems that there's a coolness between them. After all, it was her husband who was the friend.

Jean thinks of Sandy Cargill's words- and how Etienne will feel being under the same roof as the widow of the man who sold him?

Chapter 25

4th September, 1790
Paris

Jacob has a headache and would much prefer to get on with his correspondence and have an early night. Mirabeau has other ideas, and instead, they are in a side room of the National Constituent Assembly, with Necker and two of the deputies, whom they regard as trustworthy. There's a scratch supper of bread, cheese and fruit, on the sideboard, and their half empty glasses of wine are on the table, along with the papers they've been discussing.

The week before, the finance minister offered his resignation before he was sacked and the Treasury is now under the control of the Assembly. Necker left for his country estates at Vesoul but was arrested and brought back. Tomorrow, he will leave France, possibly for good, but before he does so, this small gathering needs to consult him on the state of the country's finances.

He sits back in his chair, coat unbuttoned to show a richly embroidered waistcoat- his one vanity. He flips open his enamelled pocket watch to squint at the time. The problem, he declares is that the Assembly's insistence on the Assignat paper money being the full value of the Church property and not as he wanted only a quarter means there will inevitably be financial pain ahead. He's wrangled down the suggested sum to less than half the almost two billion livres. 'Had you agreed to set up a National Bank, like Paterson did for England, we would not be in such peril.'

Jacob agrees, but remembers that Paterson, who perished in the debacle of Darien, did not always enjoy such wise judgement when it came to decision making.

Necker has left two million livres of his own money with the French Treasury and Jacob suspects, the way things are going, that he will not see a penny of this back. That's a poor reward for trying to sort out a country which under the current monarch has drifted towards bankruptcy.

Mirabeau and Necker- who should be friends- are also at odds. Mirabeau is less anxious about the state of the economy, arguing that what's been politically achieved is little less than a miracle. Necker sees the drift towards paper currency with foreboding. Once he's gone, who will be strong enough to steer the Treasury?

He's leaving France- and his considerable property, including his fine house in Rue de la Chaussee d'Antin and the estate at Saint Ouen sur Seine will be confiscated. It's a poor reward for the years he's given France.

'Where will you go?' Jacob asks.

'It's been many years since I left Switzerland. Now, I think it's time I returned. My family will stay at Coppet Castle. It won't be easy. I doubt the French emigres who have settled near there will welcome me.' He gives Jacob a thin smile and indicates Mirabeau. 'Look out for my friend, there. We might not agree on much at the moment but France cannot afford to lose both of us.'

Chapter 26

October, 1790

Salons appear all over Paris, in locations as diverse as convents and theatres. As the sister-in-law of a deputy, the acquaintance of a Marquise, and the wife of a Scottish merchant, Francine finds most doors open to her and invitations extend to Sandy and to Jacob. This evening, the event is at the home of a countess, who prides herself on her wide circle of friends, and has dropped her title to style herself a citizen. Sandy has business elsewhere and Jacob is taking his place for the evening.

Jacob takes a turn around the room with Francine on his arm and recognises Olympe des Gouges in conversation with two deputies of the Assembly. Her voice is raised, and Jacob suspects she is talking about the outrage in Saint Domingue over the closure of the Assembly in Hispaniola. The National Assembly has dropped the idea of the abolition of slavery. There are too many people with too much to lose, including the free men of mixed race who run plantations and often own slaves as well.

Women of the Revolution

Manon Roland, seated in an alcove is apparently engrossed in writing a letter. He smiles, knowing the woman is listening intently to the conversation and probably recording it in her missives to her husband who has returned to his post.

Marie Joseph Rose de Beauharnais, dressed in the latest fashion in a high waisted frock with flowing folds of fabric is surrounded by male admirers. She attends only those gatherings where she is unlikely to be in the company of her estranged husband, Francine tells him. He remembers her from the identification of the corpse. Lately, his attempts to find out what the man was doing have tailed off, and he makes a mental note to seek her out and ask her about the dead Antoine Deschamps, who has been laid to rest these last few months.

There is chatter in the air. The courtiers are agog with news of mutiny among the navy and the revelation that the King has written to the King of Spain about his dislike for the new status of the clergy. Some are saying that they do not trust Louis Capet not to seek help from his wife's brother, the emperor.

Curtius and his niece arrive and make their way across to where the Marquise is talking with Francine's sister and the Deschamps widow. The widow, Virginie, looks as if she is enjoying the evening. Her dress is new, she's put on some weight, which suits her, and she's laughing at something the Marquise is saying. Francine taps him on the arm with her fan and raises an eyebrow. They move closer, and Francine joins the conversation, pulling Jacob into the circle.

'How nice to see you again,' Virginie says to Jacob. Her facial muscles are smiling, but since he has joined the circle, that smile does not reach her eyes, which are cold.

'The last time was under very difficult circumstances,' he replies. He remembers her lack of emotion at the Morgue.

Might she have had a hand in Antoine's fate?

He looks round the gathering. He would normally expect to see the page, Etienne in attendance, but the boy is missing. He exchanges a look with Francine who shrugs and accepts a glass of dessert wine from the tray offered by a footman.

Francine takes a dainty sip and asks, 'Madame Deschamps, when do you plan to return to Saint Domingue?'

For a second, Jacob sees a look of horror in the eyes of Virginie Deschamps. She gives a nervous little laugh and replies, 'I plan to remain in Paris, for the time being at least. I have no family to support me at home, and the Marquise' brother has generously agreed to settle some money on me.'

That would account for her new wardrobe- she looks very different from the dowdy woman Jacob first met. He feels a tap on his arm, and Marie Grosholz whispers, 'She isn't telling the whole truth. Ask them about the Will.'

Jacob hesitates, then says, 'What brought your late husband to Paris? Was he among the delegation from Saint Domingue who wanted representation in the Assembly last year?'

She nods, then changes her mind and shakes her head. 'We travelled with them, but my husband wanted clarification about what he was left in his father's Will.'

The Marquise opens her fan and makes a gesture dismissing the group to signal the conversation is over.

It is Francine who says, 'Have you left your little page at home, Marquise? I declare this is the first time in a year I have seen you without him?'

The Marquise and Virginie Deschamps exchange a look that indicates they are uncomfortable with this suggestion. The Marquise takes her new friend by the arm, and they move to the other side of the room.

Left to themselves, Francine asks Jacob, 'What do you

think she's done with the boy?'

Marie Grosholz says 'I see widows at the Morgue who are heartbroken at their loss. I have seldom seen one as stone faced as her. Her friend's tears were real. Now, she has asked us to let her have the death mask, or to destroy it. We explained that we will always need to keep one copy of such a mask for the Morgue archives.'

'Not everyone is comfortable sharing their grief,' Jacob tells her.

It is nine months since the body was pulled from the river, and while the corpse was identified, the mystery of the man remains. Was he a spy for England? Or was he the victim of a duel that went wrong?

These thoughts are running through Jacob's mind as they circulate. He watches his friend's wife sparkle. Francine is in her element at these evenings, and her ease at joining conversations makes him feel self-conscious at his own lack of confidence. His role in the Assembly does not involve speech making but recording the words of others. As a mere official, he is out of place in such glittering company.

The evening draws to a close, and carriages and sedan chairs line up outside to take the guests home. As he hands Francine into the Geddes equipage, he catches a glimpse of Etienne, lurking at the back of the Marquise's carriage, demoted from page. The footman's livery he wears is four sizes too big for the lad, and there's a bruise on his cheek. Strange that this should happen while the Deschamp woman has insinuated herself into that household. There's a look in the boy's eyes he hasn't seen before. Fear.

Chapter 27

Jacob rides in the carriage with Francine to her house. The lit torches in their holders at each side of the front door are blazing, and through the windows, the rooms are brightly lit with beeswax candles. Jacob helps her alight and nods to the coachman to take the coach round the back to the mews. Francine offers the use of the equipage to take him home, but he reminds her that the street where he lives is too narrow for any vehicle larger than a sedan chair. Besides the night is dry and mild, and the walk will do him good.

This part of Paris has lights and there's a full moon too, so he doesn't feel concerned for his footing. In fact, after the gathering he's attended, he's glad of the chance to gather his thoughts. The presence of Virginie and the demotion of Etienne must be connected, if he could only work out how. Marie Grosholz's prompt about a Will is a clue- and didn't Virginie Deschamps mention her late husband came to Paris because of some terms of his father's Will?

He's barely round the corner when he hears footsteps behind him. Instinctively he loosens the catch on his sword cane and continues onward, without turning around. His ears are attuned, and he realises whoever is following him is taking a step when he does and stops when he stops.

He's in his best suit of clothes, which are far from opulent, but might make him a target for a casual thief. He checks for his keys, watch and the small purse of coin tucked into an inner pocket.

He keeps on walking in the direction of his house, and stops, pretending to consult his watch, while drawing the sharpened blade from the cane. When he whirls round, the follower ducks into a doorway. He doesn't see the other one, approaching from behind, who whips a bag over his head and swiftly relieves him of the blade, fastening his hands behind his back. A sharp blow to the head fells him.

He's aware of being manhandled into a sedan chair and groans as his assailants take their places at the front and back, lifting the cabin and jogging through the streets. He tries to estimate if they are turning right or left, but he feels sick from the motion, and cannot concentrate.

Do they know who he is? If these people were casual thieves, they'd have taken his valuables and left him behind, surely?

He left the Geddes house at half past ten. If he isn't back soon, Jean will need to raise the alarm.

He calls out, 'Help!' but knows the cloth bag is muffling his voice, and there's a snarl from one of his attackers to shut his mouth. He thinks of Antoine Deschamps, and wonders if this is how the man met his end- attacked by common footpads.

He tries to work his hands free from the bindings. He cannot see, but they feel like cords rather than rough twine. He succeeds in loosening them a little, but the more he struggles the harder the task is- the knots they've used are intricate. He's still trying to work at his bonds when the sedan chair is set down and he is hauled out and manhandled down a flight of steps and into a building. They rip the bag from his head, before throwing him on a hard floor. He hears a door slam and the turn of a key in a lock, before he's swallowed by darkness.

Chapter 28

Being treated as his father in law's errand boy can be a thorough nuisance, Cargill reflects, making his way through Gutter Lane. The old man insisted he collect the package from the button maker himself, rather than send a crewman.

It's half a day he cannot really afford to waste, given that Jacob also sent word that he had correspondence to collect from George Rose at the Treasury. It means that he must neglect the tasks that Jess had for him – things for her and the children that must now be left for the homeward trip.

London, as always, is teeming with life, and he's hearing an increasing number of French voices as he walks through Cheapside. The piece of paper with the address guides him to a place he last visited a decade ago, on a similar commission.

The woman behind the counter is new. He'd have remembered her before, with that fox-coloured hair and those sharp green eyes that look him up and down as if assessing his manhood. He tells her he's there to collect an order for the Half Moon plantation in Saint Domingue and she raises her eyebrows and goes into the workshop to fetch the proprietor.

The man appears a few minutes later, holding a cube shaped casket, which he sets on the counter and opens, to show the trays of engraved buttons inside. Cargill takes one out and holds a magnifying glass to his eye to check the quality of the etched design. He nods and the box is wrapped in cloth and tied with twine.

He hands over a heavy purse in exchange for the goods, and the button maker asks if he will take refreshment. He's about to decline, when the look on the proprietor's face changes his mind. 'The Lewis across the road serves a good pie with mash at this time of day.'

Cargill is about to leave the box behind, but the button maker nods to take it with them.

The innkeeper greets the button maker by name and they are soon ensconced in a booth, with food and ale in front of them. 'Is something wrong, man?' Cargill asks.

'The business is fine, Andrew,' he says, 'too fine, if you ask me.'

Cargill takes a mouthful of warm beer and plunges a fork into the food, 'What do you mean?'

'A year ago, I was working on my own in the shop. I wasn't making a fortune, but I got by and there was a small profit at the end of each week. Then back in the spring of this year, these two women walked in and offered to work for me. I had a card in the window offering a position, and I was expecting a man perhaps? Or a lad to train as an apprentice. I offered them a fortnight's trial, and the room at the back.'

'Do you feel uncomfortable having them in the business?' Cargill asks, taking a mouthful of pie. 'You're right about this pie. It's the best I've had in a long time.'

'They're good at their jobs, and the one in the shop knows how to flirt with the customers and get them to buy things, but there's something about them that I don't trust. Then there's this,' he pulls a piece of paper from his pocket and pushes it across the table to Cargill, who turns it over and reads.

'One of them is a felon?' he raises his eyebrows.

'Someone pushed that under my door. I've had government men watching the shop too, and they've been asking questions about these buttons. We've been making these since I was a lad, but this is the first time I've ever been asked about them.'

He takes a mouthful of his own food and says, 'Who exactly is this order for? It wasn't the usual instructions, and you've brought payment in coin. Am I in trouble?'

Cargill takes another drink and says, 'I can't really say. My father-in-law told me to collect the box and drop it off at Saint Domingue. I know he's trading with the plantation owners, so this is just a part of my cargo crossing the Atlantic. Believe me, I'm as much in the dark as you are.'

The other man reaches across the table to touch Cargill's arm. 'Tell me what you know about a dead man with one of these buttons in Paris. I told that government clerk who we made them for, and he said something about an investigation, but wouldn't say more. Does it have anything to do with my workers?'

Cargill shakes his head. 'I don't think so, but it looks like one of the Deschamps family was dragged out of the river Seine, near the start of the year. That's as much as I know, but I'm due to meet a man who might be able to tell me more.'

Chapter 29

Jacob comes to in a dark room. His hands are still tied behind him. He's wet himself. His head is still thumping, and he is seeing everything in duplicate. He knows this is bad. His face is pressed hard into the floor and his right arm has gone to sleep.

He's on a stone flagged floor that hasn't been scrubbed for a long time and the one tiny window has bars on it. It's still dark, so either he's not been here for a long time, or he's been unconscious for an entire day.

At least he's still alive- for the moment.

Has he been taken because of his work? He doubts that- if his capture was political, he'd be in a prison cell, and this room is more like a scullery. Judging by the state of the place it's either an empty house or one with a particularly slovenly scullery maid.

With a heroic effort he rolls onto his back, groaning as his hands are crushed under him but then manages to wriggle into a seated position. If he can shuffle towards the wall, and lean on it, he might be able to ease the pain and let his brain start to function. He badly needs a drink but all he can see, looking round the space is a pail beside the wall nearest the window.

By the time he has reached the pail, all he can do is get onto his knees, lower his head into the water and drink, lapping at the water like a dog. He's not too sure the water is fresh, but when he finally manages to lean against the wall, water still dripping from his stock, he feels a little bit better.

He's not quite up to standing, which is just as well, because the ceiling is very low, even for him, and this makes him suspect his captors have put him in a cellar.

He can't see anything to eat, but he feels as if he's going to be sick and he doubts he could keep anything down.

Jacob wonders who will miss him first? Jean will be worried- her own subsistence depends on him. Mirabeau will no doubt look for him- but would he assume illness and leave several days before sounding an alert?

Jean had mentioned an encounter with her twin at the Palais Royal. Might Jacques be up to mischief? Even he wouldn't dare to kidnap an official of the National Assembly.

At the back of his mind is the thought that the salon he attended with Francine has something to do with this. He has a memory of the child Etienne's face. Might this have something to do with him? Might the Marquise be treasonous? Or is this the work of the widow Deschamps?

Chapter 30

Cargill reaches Whitehall with only minutes to spare. The box he carries is an awkward shape and not wishing to make himself a target for footpads, he's stuffed it into his drawstring sack and slung it over his shoulder. It's easier to carry and further from the reach of a cut purse, but every time it bounces against his back he curses. He'll have bruises by nightfall. Just as well the wife put a bottle of witch hazel in the medicine chest.

He finds the door he's looking for, and the clerk on the desk sniffs as he glances at the letters from Scotland, but then rings a bell and talks in a quiet undertone to the flunkey who responds. The letters are placed on a silver tray and the servant departs, leaving the sea captain to sit on a bench below a high window.

Cargill sighs. He's used to this ritual. It's part of family tradition. While his father-in-law is a man of worth, a man of business and respected, Cargill is a Rose on his mother's side, and trusted by both George Rose and Jacob to convey the sort of correspondence that cannot be trusted to the mails. That correspondence has grown significantly over the past few years.

The flunkey returns after quarter of an hour and Cargill is shown up a decorative carved wooden staircase with highly polished bannisters to a carved wooden door to the side of a much grander double door. The larger door belongs to William Pitt the Younger. George Rose occupies a much less grand office next door.

The room smells of beeswax polish, pine from the logs burning in the grate, and ink. George rises to greet him, and they clasp hands and clap one another on the back.

'Aye, man,' George greets him. 'Fit like?'

Andrew Cargill smiles and responds, 'Nae bad. Foos your doos?'

It's the greeting of two who knew one another as small children, and in a language that Cargill doubts anyone in this building would understand. George offers refreshment and Cargill accepts. It's late enough in the day for a glass of sherry, which is poured from a decanter into a pair of solid looking bumpers. They toast each other's health.

The letters are open on the desk in front of George. He's scanned them before Cargill came in, and he's already dipping a goose feather quill into the ornamental inkstand to start his reply.

'Did you find any more out about that business Jacob was worried about?' Cargill asks. 'The dead man from the islands?'

George looks up from his writing and frowns. He's a handsome man, in his forties, with a long straight nose and determined chin, but his face is also kind, and all manner of people trust him, from naval officers like his good friend Nelson; his leader, Pitt and even the old King George.

'I sent my own clerk to Sweetings Lane yesterday, and what I'm about to tell you is for Jacob's ear alone,' he says, writing swiftly, finishing a sentence and replacing the quill in the stand.

'The Half Moon Plantations were originally entirely in the possession of the Deschamps family, of Bordeaux,' he begins. 'However, as you know, the islands in the West Indies have changed hands several times, and on the death of old Camille Deschamps, the family in France made enquiries about forming a company which would include a British partner, preferably a Scotsman. It meant that in the event of the islands falling into British hands, that the Deschamps family would not lose their property. That partner was found around twenty years ago. Perhaps you will recognise the name on this deed?' He draws a document from a folder on the desk and pushes it across to Cargill.'

The sea captain squints at the faded writing, and hands it back. 'I'd no idea of this, George. This explains a lot.'

'Your wife's late grandfather was one of those prepared to put up the money, providing the shares stayed in his family. They passed on his death to his daughter and son in law. Of course, the son in law was already trading with the Deschamps plantations, and it made perfect sense for the family to make that investment. I gather it has grown considerably over the years? It even paid for a ship?'

'My ship?' Cargill asks.

George nods and raises his glass to his lips.

'However,' he continues, 'Old Camille Deschamps was less than honest with his own family. His wife was not suited to the heat and chose to return to France. He was left to his own devices and took up with several local women. It turned out he had a few families- a son in France, Henri, who was his legitimate heir, but also children by those Creole ladies, who he put in charge to run his plantations. In turn, they passed their positions to their own sons, one of whom was Antoine Deschamps. It appears that Antoine was under the misapprehension that his father, Claud owned the plantation where they worked, and all the enslaved people on it, and he wanted to claim funds from his grandfather's estate. I believe he travelled to Paris with some other people of mixed race like himself, including a Vincent Oge? You might want to ask Jacob about what happened to the promises the Assembly made? It seems the free people of colour believed they would have full voting rights, even if they still supported slavery, being slave owners themselves?'

Cargill knows that George Rose's wife is from a slave owning family. It's set Rose apart from Pitt and Wilberforce, who want to abolish slavery. Anyone who owns slaves will fight tooth and nail to keep them- or obtain compensation, if the price is high enough. The self-interest makes Cargill uneasy.

'At any rate,' he continues, 'Oge was here in London for a while. Our intelligence agents followed him to a meeting with Thomas Clarkson before he went back to Saint Domingue. At that meeting he raised the case of a friend who he believed to be murdered in Paris who had been working for His Majesty King George's government.

Cargill finishes his whisky, barely tasting it as it burns its way down his throat. These are not comfortable truths for a man who reads pamphlets condemning slavery in his cabin on long nights at sea.

'Please tell Jacob to tread very carefully,' George says. 'The Deschamps heir- the legitimate one who owns two thirds of the Half Moon company- was not fully aware of old Camille's other families. It seems that others apart from Antoine are emerging from the woodwork to make claims on the estates and rather than settle with them he is out to destroy them- and even to return free men of colour among those kin to slavery. He is a ruthless fellow and could be dangerous if anyone gets in his way. Better to leave such matters to the police and stand back.'

He returns to his writing and finishes the letters, blotting them with sand from a silver shaker, then blowing on the papers, folding them and sealing them, using the Rose family crest, then replacing the ring on his finger.

He hands the packets to Cargill. 'When do you sail?' he asks.

'If there's a favourable wind, I hope on the morning tide. I've got business in Paris before I leave for Saint Domingue, and this will be my last voyage for the year. Home for Hogmanay, I hope.'

George walks with him down the stairs to the main door. 'I must be in Parliament for the vote tonight. I wish you a safe journey, my friend.'

Chapter 31

Jacob, leaning against the wall, beside the water pail, watches as the sun rises and projects the window bars against the opposite wall. Nobody has appeared since he woke up, and his stomach is rumbling. To his shame, he cannot even open the front of his breeches to relieve himself. The bonds might be silk cords, but the knots are intricate and the harder he struggles, the tighter they become.

At noon, the door opens and a boy with a bag over his head and hands tied behind him is also thrust into the scullery. He lands hard on his knees and yelps with pain. His assailants slam the door and bolt and lock it before Jacob has time to protest that they need food and water.

Jacob calls out, 'Let me help you, child.'

It takes some time, but the boy wriggles on his knees towards Jacob by following the sound of his voice and by careful manoeuvring, he's able to take the bag off the lad's head. It's Etienne.

Etienne says, 'I can't take my own bonds off, but if we sit back to back, we might be able to free each other?'

He's right, Jacob realises, working on the child's bonds.

It's easier to free the other. The moment the boy's hands are free, he shakes them vigorously and then unties Jacob, who breathes a huge sigh of relief.

'What did they do to you, Etienne? And why are you in here?'

Etienne looks as if he wants to burst into tears. There are a few heaving sobs, but he fights against them and finally says, 'Madam Antoine wants me gone. She told my mistress that I was a liar and a thief, and I should be sent to the plantation fields and not be a page anymore.'

'Your mistress the Marquise?'

The child is miserable. Jacob recalls seeing him arrive on that cart with Cargill, a year and a half ago. A little boy, poorly clad, missing his mother. The Marquise bought him as her page, dressed him in fine livery and kept him by her side, only to drop him when another pet came her way.

'She sent me to listen at doors and come back and tell her what the servants said about her. She made me spy on her friends. I did what she told me to do. Everyone in her house hated me because I did these things and they called me a sneak.'

Now, the child is an outcast. Why has he been put in here? Jacob wonders who ordered their imprisonment. He's never liked the Marquise and he's spoken to Sandy and Francine about his mistrust. He suspects she is on Marat's list of treasonous aristocrats, plotting to overthrow the revolution.

Able to stand now, Jacob is aware of how low the ceiling really is. He's not a very tall man- but he isn't short either, and there is barely six inches between the crown of his head and the beams. There's not enough room for him to stretch. There's a rough table and several stools in the corner, and he pulls these into the middle of the space and invites Etienne to sit down. Free to move around, he looks for a cup and finds one. This means they can share the remains of the water. He fills the cup and hands it to the boy, who gulps the water and wipes his hand across his face.

Neither man nor boy knows when the door will open again, and what their fate might be. Jacob wishes he knew the location of their prison, and if his absence has been noticed yet.

He can only hope that Jean has already gone for help.

Chapter 32

Jean comes down the stairs in the morning, yawning, rubbing sleep from her eyes, but ready to kindle the fire in the basement scullery and get the porridge pot ready. She's used to Jacob moving around in the rooms upstairs as he does his ablutions and gathers his things for the day. The first thing she's aware of is how quiet it is.

On her knees, she rakes out yesterday's ashes, and twists paper into spills. She uses the flints and gets the sparks to light the papers, before feeding the fire with sticks and adding fuel. She goes into the yard to fetch water from the well. The little bucket comes up full and she fills the ewer, taking it into the scullery to mix water into the oatmeal. She will refill the upstairs jugs after breakfast.

There's still no sound of movement, so she climbs the stairs and taps on Jacob's door. There's no response, so she opens the door. His bed hasn't been slept in. It's made neatly, with the blankets so tightly tucked in that you could bounce a coin on them.

Perhaps he stayed at the Geddes house yesterday evening? If so, he will need his papers, and he will return to collect them before he goes to the Assembly. She tells herself that there's no reason to worry, but she's uneasy and goes through the motions of her daily tasks, telling herself he will arrive home soon.

Jean sets about making the porridge, and she takes the coffee beans she roasted yesterday, grinds them and puts them into the pot, adds water and sets the pot on the stove.

By the time Jean has breakfasted, done her household chores and taken money from the cash box to go and buy bread, she's starting to be anxious.

She comes back from market to find the house still empty. There's work for her to complete this morning, but instead she sets off for the Geddes house.

Sandy is at his desk, writing letters. Francine, sitting on a chair in his study, still in her wrapper, is sipping chocolate and she looks up when Jean is shown in.

'Has Jacob left for the Assembly yet? I've brought his satchel.' Jean asks.

'Jacob went home last night,' Francine begins, 'Wasn't he with you this morning? He left us to walk home.'

She sees the stricken look on the clerk's face. Sandy sets his quill down, stands up and says to Francine, 'Didn't you offer the carriage, my dear?'

'He said it's too wide for his street, and he wanted the exercise,' Francine replies in a small voice.

'Think, my dear. Who might wish our friend harm?' He calls for his coat and cane and when they are brought, Francine helps him put them on. He kisses her cheek then turns to Jean. 'We shall retrace his steps and see if he's left us any clues as to where he's gone.'

They set off- the merchant carrying a walking staff; the clerk pacing beside him. Jean knows the route well, having taken it with Jacob many times. They turn the corner into the narrower street, and halfway down, she spots something- the case of the sword cane. The handle with the blade is missing. She shows it to Sandy Geddes, and he says, 'This is bad. He drew the blade to fend off an attacker.'

He goes to the nearest house and thumps on the door with his staff. A serving woman appears, alarmed by the noise and asks what he wants. She holds the door, scared they will barge their way in, but Sandy asks, 'Did you see a commotion outside? About ten o clock last night? A friend of ours has been taken, and we are concerned for his safety.'

She nods, and says, 'I will ask my mistress,' and disappears into the hallway, to reappear with her employer, a woman of middle age who is alarmed by the strangers at the door, until Sandy introduces himself as a neighbour from the next street.

They repeat their questions, and the lady of the house shakes her head. 'I was in bed by nine o clock, and my bedchamber is at the back of the building. You might try across the road? They're always late home. They might have seen something?'

At the third house, a servant tells them he heard a noise, and saw a sedan chair depart in a hurry. 'The chairmen looked a pair of blackguards and ruffians.'

'Did you see which direction they went in?' Jean asks. The servant indicates the junction and says, 'That leads to the river.'

Jean is thinking of Antoine Deschamps, and his watery fate.

If Jacob has been killed, what will become of her?

Chapter 33

The time passes slowly and still nobody comes. Jacob and Etienne are seated at the table. Jacob has recovered his composure a little, although the smell of piss on his best breeches makes him feel unclean.

He's pressed his face to the little window and from the proximity of the wall opposite he's sure they are in the basement of a house. Not a prison as such, then. He carefully questions the boy, about where he was when he was taken, and how long it took his kidnappers to bring him here. He needs to know if they are still in Paris, and where in the city they might be.

Their assailants took care to cover their victims' faces and prevent them seeing the route, which leads him to believe this was a premeditated act.

One pail of water and no food suggests that while they are not intended to die, they are not being left in any comfort either.

He's checked the door. He might be able to pick the lock if he can find a knife somewhere, but it is also bolted. Perhaps brute force might be required? He doesn't know if his captors are nearby and if he fails, he doesn't much like the idea of having his hands retied. Besides, he's got the boy to think of. If they are to escape, they must do so together and they cannot risk being retaken.

He questions Etienne, 'Why were you on the carriage last night? Did you see anything that was unusual?'

The Marquise knows where Francine Geddes lives- there would have been no need to follow their carriage, but Etienne confirms that their carriage, with the Marquise and Madam Antoine inside, detoured to pass the house. That suggests that she might have ordered his abduction, but why? It is a huge risk to attack an official of the Assembly, particularly one who has worked with Necker and Mirabeau.

Might they be prisoners of a political club like the Cordeliers? That's less likely because they would have made themselves known, by coming in and ranting about their politics. Marat wouldn't be able to stay away without dropping by for an argument.

They are not prisoners of the state. He can all but rule out political abduction. That leaves a more sinister option.

'Etienne, what can you tell me about Madam Antoine Dechamps?' Jacob asks, trying to keep his voice calm and level.

The child is distressed, but he takes a deep breath and tells Jacob his story.

Etienne lived with his mother, Lucia, the cook, below stairs at Half Moon Plantation in Saint Domingue. His father, the boss, Claud, was the son of Camille, and his island wife, Maria, a Creole lady. Claud was married to Antoine's mother, the daughter of another plantation owner. They had Antoine and two daughters, who married on the island. As Claud's son, Antoine was sent to school in Martinique to be educated as a gentleman. He became friends with the children of prominent French and British families in the islands. Antoine's mother died three years before Etienne was born and Claud took Lucia to his bed.

Jacob thinks back to the Morgue and the reactions of Rose Beauharnais, who had known Antoine from her schooldays in Martinique, and shed the tears he would expect from a widow.

Antoine might have been educated as a gentleman, but a match with Rose, whose parents expected their daughter to make a glittering alliance, was out of the question. Instead he married Rose's classmate, the orphaned Virginie de la Croix, and from the moment she arrived she set out to take control of her husband, her father-in-law, the household and the plantation. She took a particular dislike to Lucia, even more so when Claud told her that Lucia and Etienne were free, and not enslaved and that he intended to send the boy to school in Martinique- the same school that Antoine had attended. To ensure their security, their papers were lodged with a notary on the island, in case there was any confusion in the event of Claud's death. Claud made that very clear to Lucia, who knew where to seek out the lawyer.

Master Claud died in 1788 from a very sudden illness and from that moment, Virginie, calling herself the mistress of Half Moon, assumed command. She wanted to change the house, which still had the furnishings of forty years before, and above all, she wanted rid of that woman downstairs and her son.

Lucia offered to seek work elsewhere, if Antoine kept his promise to send Etienne to school, and if she had her own papers to show a new employer that she was indeed a free woman.

Within days, the lawyer's office was set on fire, and the precious documents were lost. The notary, who had drawn them up, perished in the fire. Now, Virginie denied their freedom and declared she would sell both mother and son.

Julie MP Adams

Etienne saw his mother in chains, sold to another plantation on the same day he was packed off to France, a prisoner on Captain Cargill's ship. His mother wailed when he was taken on board and he called out to her that he would return one day to save her.

'I said I would come back. Sir, how can I do so now?' The pain in the child's voice steals its way into Jacob's heart.

When they were at sea a day, the Captain came down to the hold where the child had a hammock and took him up on deck to get some fresh air. He found out that Etienne could read and write, and he got him to write a letter to his mother. He said he would find out where she was and take the letter to her on his next voyage.

When, after weeks at sea, they reached France, Cargill delivered the child to the Versailles house of a friend of the Marquise and bade him farewell. However, on his next visits to France he brought notes from Lucia and collected the letters that Etienne wrote in return. The boy looked forward to those exchanges at the kitchen door, where he got precious news of his mother, and he used his few moments alone to draft what he would say in the next missive until there was a change in the household.

'Madam Antoine arrived and a week ago told Milady that she caught me stealing paper and ink and I was a bad person.' As Etienne remembers this, a cloud comes over his face. The newcomer said she knew how to deal with wicked slaves and she had him beaten until he begged for mercy.

The other servants didn't like him- but none of them had informed on him before, when he took a precious sheet of paper or filched a goose quill. The cook, took pity on him when she found him locked in the cellar, crying, and let him up to the kitchen, and fed him bread and jam. A maid found salve for his wounds.

'What is Madam Antoine's status in the house?' Jacob

asks the lad.

'She is Milady's companion,' Etienne tells him, 'But I heard her tell the Marquis that they are keeping her where they can watch her. Milady's brother, Henri Deschamps is angry with Madam Antoine. He says she tries to blackmail him.'

'Did you ever hear her say why they came to Paris?' Jacob watches the boy carefully. By his own admission, Etienne has become expert at listening at doors. Jean told him as much.

'Antoine wanted the papers to prove he owned Half Moon estate.' Etienne shrugs. 'But Henri Deschamps said that Grandfather Camille was not married to Grandmother Maria because he was married already to Milady's grandmother. Henri Deschamps owns Half Moon.'

Antoine had inherited a job, not a plantation, and his wife was shocked to learn they had no money at all- not even the coins for their passage home. Told that Half Moon was owned by a company whose partners included Deschamps and a British merchant, Antoine went on board Cargill's ship bound for England and was not seen again until he was pulled from the river.

A chill runs down Jacob's spine. It sounds as if Antoine was conveniently disposed of, whether by the Marquise and her brother, or his own discontented wife, who would need her freedom to seek a new, richer husband in Paris. Worse still, the last person to see him alive was Cargill. Surely his good friend is not a murderer?

Chapter 34

Jean returns to the office exhausted. Her feet ache and she has walked miles since this morning, She and Sandy followed in Jacob's footsteps, through streets and side alleys, asking all the while if anyone had seen the sedan chair last night, but after four hours, the trail was cold. Instead, they trailed back, looking for signs that were not there.

Sandy Geddes has finally gone to Mirabeau to seek his advice and tell him of his friend's danger. Mirabeau has the authority to order an official search, but if Jacob's life is in danger, the police may not be in time.

Jean tries to settle to work, but her mind refuses to focus, and finally she snatches up her jacket and makes her way through the dark streets to the Cordelier district. Jacques is staying with Marat, and she finds both at the Cordeliers Club where they are arguing over the contents of the next edition of the People's Friend. She is loathe to ask her twin for anything, but they have exhausted every other line of enquiry. It is late in the evening by the time she gets there, and a meeting is in process. She is half surprised to see that many of the men and women sitting in the refectory are soberly dressed clerks like herself. She's heard them described as radical ruffians.

Jacques raises his eyebrows at his twin. 'Why, if it isn't Jean the clerk come to a political club? Can we make a good citizen of you, Jean?'

Judging from the jug on the table, which is more than half full, he hasn't been drinking too much, and she needs him to have a clear head. 'Jacob's been kidnapped. What do you know about it?'

He almost falls off his seat but recovers his composure and pulls out a stool for her. 'Sit down.' He pours wine into a cup and thrusts it at her. 'Drink this and tell me what's happened.'

Marat is listening carefully, as she tells them that Jacob set out for home but was attacked and bundled into a sedan chair. 'I found his sword cane. He could have fought one off, but he was ambushed. Does he have enemies we should worry about?'

Others have gathered round. There's general agreement among the lawyers present that Jacob Rose is a sound fellow, without an enemy among the political clubs, and he's respected even by the churchmen.

Jacques says, 'And what about the aristocrats? Marat, where's that list of yours?'

She's heard talk of the list of potentially treasonous nobles, but this is the first time she has seen it, and it is twenty pages long, with the names and reasons why they should be executed.

There are names Jean recognises as senior members of the court, close to King Louis, but Jacques tells her to look for people with whom Jacob has had business dealings or recently seen.

'Think, Jean, where was Jacob yesterday evening?'

She tells him of the invitation to the salon the previous

evening and he clicks his fingers and calls out to a man who has recently come in. He crosses to him, and Jean sees her twin in a different light. There's an urgent exchange of words, and he returns to their table. 'Jacob was in conversation with Henri Deschamps's sister, the Marquise, and her new companion, the widow Deschamps. Robert, there attended with Madame Roland, and he saw them.'

'Have they taken him?' Jean wonders if she can persuade Francine to visit the Marquise and take her along. If he's held in the house, they might find him.

Marat gulps his wine. 'If they have him, it won't be in their own home. They'll keep him somewhere else.'

Jean shudders, thinking of the terrifying days when she was held in the rat-infested attic of the Gregoire house.

'Leave it to us. We have spies in the houses on the list. We'll find where they're holding him. Wait here.'

Jean protests that it would be better for her to return home, but her twin says, 'If Jacob is in danger, you might well be too. You're safer here, with other people around.'

Chapter 35

Cargill's ship docks at Le Havre, and he supervises the offloading of the cargo he will take into Paris. It's a two-day journey on the road by cart, and he'll stop at an inn on the way, to dine and sleep, and be up at the crack of dawn to reach the city before nightfall. He has George Rose's letters on his person, and he will need to keep them safe. It wouldn't do for anyone to learn about the correspondence between Jacob and George: even if the two men are kin, it could endanger them.

He's still turning George's revelation about the ownership of Half Moon Plantations over in his head. It shocks him to realise that through his marriage, he has a more direct connection to the plantations than he realised. He's always known Jessamine's father plays his cards close to his chest, but this is the first he's heard of it.

When he reaches the inn, there's a message waiting for him. The landlord who shows him up to the private room where he will dine and sleep, brings the packet along with a flagon of house wine, and says he will send the girl up to light the stove. He's so weary he could throw himself into bed and sleep, but he needs to eat. The candles are lit, and while the maid lights the logs in the little stove, and the innkeeper's wife bustles in with his supper, he breaks the seal and reads.

His first impulse is to say he must be on his way with neither bed nor board, but his body tells him he will be of no use if he drops from fatigue on the road and thieves take his cargo and the documents. Instead, he sits at the table, and forks cassoulet into his mouth, thinking of his friend and who might wish him ill. He might as well be eating paper, for he tastes nothing of the meal in his haste to finish.

He's a creature of habit, and used to life on the high seas, he can usually fall into a deep sleep wherever he can find a place to lay his head, but on this night, he's tormented by bad dreams, and wakes, with the faces of his friend and kinsman Jacob and the child Etienne in his mind.

Chapter 36

Night falls and nobody has brought food or water. Jacob bundles his best jacket up and makes a rough pillow. They will be sleeping on the cold flags and it's a choice between warmth or a sore head. Once he's sure their captors are not nearby he will attempt to break the door at first light. The pail is half empty now, and they won't last without water or sustenance.

He needs to use a privy, but there's nothing that will serve as a chamber pot. He gets up and prowls around, trying to stretch and striking his knuckles on the beams.

The first thing that alarms him is a crackling sound from above his head. He crosses to the window and sees a red glow reflected in the alleyway. The house above them is on fire. He rips his stock off, tears it in two, and soaks both pieces in what is left of the water, wrapping one part round his nose and mouth and handing the other to the sleepy Etienne to do the same.

He doesn't have time to pick the lock- he will need to break the door of their cell open. He takes six paces back and charges at it but succeeds only in hurting his shoulder. The wretched door might as well be six feet thick steel. He kicks hard but does little more than splinter the foot of door. Etienne has found a bit of metal and sets to trying to pick the lock on the door, and all the while, serpents of smoke are insinuating their way through the joists into the cellar.

The smoke stings and reddens their eyes, and makes their efforts even more painful.

Jacob thinks of Jean, who will be worrying not only about him, but about her own future. He wishes he had made provision for her. He thinks of all of those who depend upon him, from Mirabeau at the Assembly to Geddes and Cargill. Have they noted his absence? Is anyone looking for him?

Etienne calls, 'I've sprung the lock. It's just the bolt now. Try to kick it open again.'

Jacob kicks hard, but the door remains stubbornly intact.

The boy yells 'Help!' but Jacob knows the noise of the fire will drown out his voice.

Feebly, Jacob runs at the door again and again. There's a slight give in it, but the bolt outside still holds.

The glass in the window shatters- blown out by heat, and just as Jacob is giving up, the door swings open and a young ruffian grabs him under his arms and hauls him outside, while another man, who looks oddly familiar hoists Etienne over his shoulder.

They are rushed up a narrow stone stair to street level, and from across a road in a poor part of the city, they watch the bones of the townhouse surrender to the fire and its rafters, glowing like a crown of rubies against the flames sink gracefully into the basement.

The knowledge of how close their brush with death has been shakes Jacob Rose to the core.

The conflagration's tendrils reach out to burn their faces, but Etienne has started to shiver. The lad's teeth are chattering, and he shakes, until he finally bursts into tears.

Chapter 37

Jacob wants his rescuers to take him home, but Jacques says that whoever imprisoned and tried to kill him might try again, if they stayed nearby to watch the house burn. Jean is at the Cordeliers club, and they've given her a room there for the night. They take him to join the clerk. Jacob is glad to be able to stretch his legs and get some blood back into his arms, and the long walk, in the company of the Cordelier radicals, allows him to listen to their ideas. The child, Etienne, is half asleep and two of the younger men catch him as he falls, several times along the way. They are closer to the river than he realised, on the other side from Notre Dame. He suspects Antoine might have spent a night in the same cellar, and shudders at the thought of what might have been his fate.

Finally, in the small hours of the morning, they stumble into the old convent, where others are waiting for them, with food and drink for the rescue party.

It's all Jean can do not to fall into Jacob's arms from the sheer relief that he's alive and relatively unscathed, apart from a scorched shirt, soot-stained skin and some small burns on his hands. Jacques and his friends got to the house just in time. The child Etienne is there too, and he looks even more terrified than before, as food and drink is set in front of him, with Marat ordering him to eat. Marat is a frightening sight at the best of times, but when he is attempting to be kind, it is disconcerting.

Jacob wants to know how they knew where to find him, and Jacques tells him that the servants of the Marquise told him about a house in a bad district where one of them had followed Madam Antoine. Once Etienne was out of favour, they realised that Milady's new spy was potentially much more dangerous. One of them had seen her outside that building with two ruffians, and she was handing money to them and giving them instructions.

Jacob thinks of the fire raisers that set Paris theatres alight throughout the past year. The child Etienne told him of the fire that conveniently destroyed the papers that would prove him and his mother to be free. Might Virginie Deschamps have something to do with other crimes? He looks across to where Etienne is sitting with a cup of milk and a hunk of bread in front of him, not yet able to eat, despite two days of starvation.

He's learned a lot from the child, and the next time he sees Raynal or Olympe des Gouges, he will listen much more attentively.

CHAPTER 38

Cargill arrives at the Geddes house to find everything in a state of disarray. Sandy is pacing the floor, while Francine has taken to her bed, weeping, wringing her hands and blaming herself for what has happened. 'If I had not persuaded him to go to the salon with me, Jacob would be safe in his own house. If harm has come to him, I can never forgive myself.'

Sandy assures her that the police are now scouring Paris for the missing Usher and that he will be found soon, but his voice lacks conviction.

He draws Cargill into his study and the two men are at a loss for what to say to one another. There is a distinct possibility that Jacob might be dead. They go through the motions of the usual paperwork that accompanies the regular visits, and Cargill asks after Jean. He will call on the clerk later in the day.

They can hear someone rap on the front door and the footman coming up from the servants' quarters to deal with the visitor. Sandy is minded to tell them to go away, but this might be someone with news of Jacob, and he calls out an instruction to show whoever it is in.

At first it appears that Jean the clerk has come to call- but this person, who looks like the clerk is taller and self-assured. He introduces himself as Jacques Rose.

'My twin and Jacob are at the Cordeliers Convent. We took them back with us overnight. The people who took Jacob prisoner already tried to kill him once, and at least with us, nobody would dare to try again the same night.'

Cargill realises he is looking at the boy he took to Paris almost two years ago, who has turned into a man. The resemblance between the siblings is clear, in the eyes and the determined chin.

Sandy invites him to sit and offers refreshment in the form of coffee which he accepts.

'Who had Jacob?' Sandy asks. Privately he wouldn't put it past the Cordeliers Club to seize the Usher for their own ends but given that deputies including Robespierre and Danton are members, perhaps not this time.

'We think it is Henri Deschamps, the owner of the Half Moon Plantations who ordered his capture. It seems the widow of Antoine, who ran the Saint Domingue estate, has been working for him, causing chaos in the city. They took Jacob because he was asking questions about Antoine's death. Henri had paid the police to make the matter go away. He didn't want the case re-opened.'

Jacques gives a grim smile. 'You read Marat's list of treacherous aristocrats? Henri Deschamps name is on it, along with his sister the Marquise and her husband. Your wife would do well to avoid their company for your own safety.

He glances at the clock on the mantel. 'I need to return. Jacob and my twin will not be safe until Virginie Deschamps is under lock and key. Danton has gone to the Assembly and will tell Mirabeau what has happened, but someone needs to stand guard in case they try again.'

He departs, leaving the two men to mull over the news. 'I didn't think I'd be glad to set eyes on that young man,' Sandy says, 'but he's saved Jacob.'

'Thank goodness,' Cargill agrees. Now appears to be a good time to break a confidence and he shares the intelligence he had from George, in London.

'We can wait until we speak with Jacob, but I have an idea how we might put a stop to Henri Deschamp's villainy, with a little help from my wife's father.'

Chapter 39

November, 1790

The fleur de lys standard flies over the Tuileries Palace for the last time as the flag of France. Last month the Assembly declared it would be replaced by the tricolour, and a crowd in the streets below watch as the flag of monarchy is lowered. For a few moments it flies at half-mast.

Anyone who does not read the papers might think the King is dead and while the flag pauses, a few old souls in the crowd ask others what is going on? Should they have come out today in mourning? The moment passes and the flag is at the foot of the pole, and the soldiers are raising the new emblem of France. There's applause from the crowd, and the King and Queen, standing on the palace balcony are expressionless. For centuries that flag has stood for the authority of an absolute monarch. Louis knows it is more than a symbol to have it replaced. It is a declaration that he is superfluous and can be removed or replaced at a moment's notice.

Word has got out that he's been writing letters to his

fellow monarchs across Europe, begging for troops, or for intervention. There are spies in the palace. How else would news of his correspondence, sent with trusted courtiers have got out?

Still, he consoles himself, the Assembly is already finding out that insurrection at home is a virus that is spreading to the overseas colonies. First Martinique, now Isle de France and Saint Domingue are having their own uprisings. The slaves in the latter island are demanding an end to their bondage. With mutiny in the army and navy, France is already overstretched.

He glances at Marie Antoinette, whose quiet hauteur is her armour against fear. Truth be told they are both terrified. It is just over a year since they left Versailles – the only home they had- for this place. They were driven- yes, that's the only word for it- by harpies and toothless peasants from the Sun King's palace to this place, where there were no rooms prepared and half the court kept their distance, slipping away one by one into exile as emigres.

His old aunts, the Mesdames, who had been living quietly at Bellevue, have travelled close to the south-east border, prepared to go into exile in Italy. He half wishes he could join them. The life of Charles I of England, that most ill-fated of monarchs, still sits on his desk, and passages from the book are all too familiar.

He disagrees with the clergy being required to swear an oath of allegiance to the Nation the Law and the King. He's said as much in his secret correspondence with Mirabeau- notes between them are conveyed by La Marck, a courtier trusted by the Queen. Mirabeau tells Louis to stand back from politics and assume the position of the Hanoverian Kings of Britain, who leave politics to those elected to run the country.

Pah! Those elected to the National Constituent

Julie MP Adams

Assembly are verbose and lack experience. All he needs to do is finish the letter he's started to the King of Prussia, and hope that help will come.

CHAPTER 40

The Marquise and her husband depart for their estates and leave behind a skeleton household. They do not invite Virginie Deschamps to join them. Henri, brother of the Marquise, confronted by Mirabeau and Jacob makes the decision to travel to Scotland. The papers he secures for the journey confirm he travels on family business, to meet with an investor.

Virginie Deschamps, has found life with her hosts extremely limiting of late, confined to the house by day and night, with windows and doors locked against her when she attempts to venture out. She has railed against such restrictions. The Marquise told her that terrible crimes have happened in Paris of late, and the locks and vigilance are for their own safety.

On those rare occasions she does go out, she is accompanied by her hostess or a servant at all times, and unable to give her guards the slip.

However, tonight, Virginie is invited to a small gathering at Pentemont Abbey. She dresses carefully for the evening. It is a chance for her to show her husband's friend Rose how her fortunes have changed. She opens a lacquered box that holds her jewels- those few inexpensive baubles she arrived with; the pieces her new friend the Marquise has gifted her, and the jewels she's acquired from her little enterprise, with the two men she met in Paris soon after her arrival. She picks up a riviere necklace of sapphires- stones of excellent quality – taken from the home of an émigré who left half of her belongings behind. Of course, Martin and Hubert, her partners in crime, set the place alight to cover their tracks.

If she wears the necklace, Rose will pass a comment and she will need to say it is mere paste. She sighs, and instead fastens the cameo pendant round her neck, and pushes the wires of the drop earrings that match it into the holes in her lobes. Most of the furniture in the Marquise' mansion is covered by dust sheets, but she uncovers a tall mirror in the entrance hall and admires her reflection. Her hair is done in Rose's favourite style, left unpowdered, caught up in a high chignon and held in place with ivory combs. She's blackened her lashes and rouged her cheeks. Yes, she'll do. She pulls the Marquise's favourite fine silk fringed shawl over her shoulders and tells the one footman left in the place that he will be required to wait up for her.

There's a hired cabriolet at the foot of the steps and she trips lightly down towards it in her velvet slippers, turning to look back at the big house she calls home. Living here, even as one dependent on the kindness of strangers, means she can look for a richer husband than her poor, deluded Antoine. The coachman hands her into the carriage, where she warms her feet on the heated brick wrapped in cloth, and they trundle off through the Paris streets, forcing pedestrians out of their way.

The note, from Rose, was a welcome surprise. She's been alone in the house, apart from the footman and kitchen maid, for a fortnight, and the maid's repertoire runs to servant food- stews, broth and the odd heavy pudding. Rose keeps an excellent table, and there will be some gentlemen in attendance also. It's good to look one's best, she decides.

The carriage stops at the side entrance, and she's helped to alight by Marie Lannoy, the faithful personal maid, sent to show her up to Rose Beauharnais' suite of rooms. She's mildly annoyed. Surely the invitation was for dinner and a salon meeting. The apartment table can only accommodate half a dozen guests. Perhaps she need not have taken such care with her toilette?

Still, if dinner is to her hostess' usual standard, it's better than sitting by the fireside with a bowl of soup and a novel.

At the top of the stairs, Marie opens the door to the dining room, announces her and then slips away. The table is set for four, and she looks round at the other diners. Rose, of course, and two men, one of whom she never expected to set eyes on again.

Jacob pulls out her chair and she sits down. The other man does likewise for Rose, and they take their places.

'I thought we'd dine early,' Rose says, but there's a hesitancy in her speech, 'and that will let you tell me what exactly happened to Antoine.'

'This gentleman,' says Jacob, 'is a prefect of the city police. A fortnight ago, they arrested two men in the act of breaking into a house near the Louvre. They'd been given the address by one who knew the owners had left France as emigres. It appears they were given such information in exchange for part of the stolen property. It was far from a first offence, and they sang like canaries when they were caught, and named their partner in crime. Whose name do you think they gave the police?'

Virginie gets to her feet, 'Excuse me, Rose, but I feel unwell, and I would like to go home.'

'Sit down, Virginie,' Jacob commands. 'If you return to

the Marquise' home you will find the door barred against you.'

Hubert and Martin, already charged with attempted murder, arson and robbery, and facing the Guillotine have expressed a preference for the galleys or hard labour. In exchange, they've given a full and frank account of their misdemeanours.

The first course, of soup is served by a maid, who exchanges a smile with Jacob, before she passes round a plate of bread, and then returns to the kitchen.

Rose lifts her spoon to her mouth, and the others follow suit. Virginie's spoon clatters against the side of the exquisitely decorated plate.

'Four weeks ago, I was abducted and taken to an address where I was held captive, along with a young boy. I would have enjoyed having a meal as good as this one,' Jacob says, helping himself to another piece of bread from the platter left on the table by the maid. 'Instead, we had a pail of water and a day spent locked in a cell, waiting for the men who took us to return and finish us off by setting the building alight. There were witnesses- and before you deny it, the prefect has their written affidavits. You were seen at that address along with Hubert and Martin and money changed hands.'

One after another, they finish the soup and set down their spoons. Only Virginie's soup is uneaten. The maid returns to clear the plates, and as she goes back into the kitchen, Virginie sees a young man standing in the doorway, listening to what is being said. She looks round wildly for any possible way out of this interrogation, but there is none.

By the time the main course, of roasted pigeon with cream and mushrooms is served, along with a dish of creamed potatoes and carrots, she can feel her heart in her throat. Her mouth is so dry she cannot swallow anything.

Women of the Revolution

Jacob pours a glass of wine for her and instructs her to drink. She takes a sip and almost chokes.

The prefect cuts up his meat with the precision of a surgeon and loads his fork, raising it to his mouth with obvious enjoyment. Rose is toying with her food and Jacob, after a mouthful of pigeon breast, takes a drink from his own glass and says, 'How exactly did Antoine die, Virginie?'

She clamps her lips together and shakes her head vigorously. Her plate is untouched.

'Here's what your henchmen told us. Antoine owed a great deal of money. He was fond of a game of cards?' This is directed to Rose, who sighs and nods. 'He came to Paris in the hope of claiming ownership of Half Moon on Saint Domingue through the courts and using it as security against a loan to clear his gambling debts. The lawyers he engaged found the claim spurious and told him to cut his losses and return home. However, the estate, along with others on Martinique and Saint Lucia is owned not by one man, but by a company, with two thirds of the shares held by Henri Deschamps, and the other third by a Scottish partner. Claud Deschamps, who used his own sons to manage the plantations, was never more than a hired manager. He owned nothing, and when Antoine learned of this, he challenged Henri to a duel.'

She looks at her food, and finally lifts her fork, cramming meat into her mouth. This will be the last meal she will probably eat, and she's damned if they are going to take her to the Conciergerie on an empty stomach. 'You know all this? Where does it say I had anything to do with it?'

Jacob continues, in the same level and reasonable voice, 'Henri Deschamps is a very skilled swordsman. His sparring partner at his school was none other than Joseph Bologna, the Chevalier de Saint Georges. St Georges acted as Henri's second. It was the work of a few moments to disarm

Antoine, tell him he no longer had a job, and leave. However, you knew how deeply indebted your husband was, and this meant you were both destitute.'

'Of course, you could cover your tracks, and you told us you saw him leave for England on a ship a day or so before the duel. But the man who got on the ship bound for England was Martin, not your spouse. Martin wore Antoine's spare set of clothes and the passage was booked in your husband's name.'

How has he found this out? She looks around the table, meeting Rose's shocked gaze. The prefect, still eating with obvious relish, is listening carefully.

Jacob lifts his glass to his mouth. He takes a drink then sets the glass down.

'You'd already met Hubert and Martin, and Antoine had lost money to them at cards and couldn't pay up. They roughed him up a little, to scare him, and you went to see them, to protest. They laughed at you for putting up with such a man, and you hatched a plan. You followed your husband to the appointed place for the duel and you waited until Henri had finished with him. Then your new friends crept up behind him and strangled him. You slashed his arms to make it look as if he had died in the fight, and then you put him into the river.'

He looks her directly in the face. 'This is what you did, Virginie?'

She starts to shake her head, 'I saw him leave on that ship. I tell you that when I saw him, he was alive.'

The prefect has finished his main course and set his knife and fork down carefully. 'The sea captain regularly visits Paris. He was here soon after your thugs tried to kill Jacob Rose and your husband's half-brother. We showed him your husband's death mask and he confirmed that the man travelling under his name was not the subject of that mask.

the duel was the day before that ship sailed and not the day after, as you maintained. We took the captain to the prison where he identified his passenger as Martin.'

The maid returns and clears the dishes. The final course, fruit and cheese, is set on the table. 'Thank you, Lucette, that will be all for this evening,' Rose Beauharnais says.

'Henri Deschamps also confirms that he left your husband very much alive. The surgeon who examined Antoine pointed out the ligature marks and the lack of water in the stomach and lungs which ruled out drowning as the cause of death. He also said that the slashes on the arms were inflicted post mortem. Dead men do not bleed.'

'However, Virginie, you were greedy. You know that there are laws against duelling and you told Henri Deschamps that you would report both the Chevalier and him for challenging Antoine, even though you knew it was the other way round. You demanded money at first, and then you forced him to place you in his sister's household, where you spied on her. I have a letter here stating that you blackmailed the Marquise.'

The prefect of police loads his plate with a chunk of Roquefort, a fig, and some grapes and accepts a glass of dessert wine. Rose, cutting her fig into four pieces, meets Virginie's eyes and says, 'Why? Why kill him? You could have come to me if you needed help. You only had to ask.'

She finds her voice. 'Yes, of course, he only had to ask, didn't he? How do you think I felt, all those years, being second best to the wonderful Rose? The one who was too good to marry him, but always kept him around, dancing attendance on you? What sort of help was that to me?'

It is almost a relief when Jacob and the prefect escort her down the stairs to the closed carriage waiting below. Her last supper sticks in her throat.

Epilogue

29th December, 1790

Henri Deschamps has had a terrible journey, but Captain Cargill kept his promise to be home for Hogmanay.

Scotland, as a Presbyterian country has no truck with Christmas, regarded by the Kirk as frivolous Papist nonsense. Unless the twenty fifth of December falls on the Sabbath, it is a normal working day, unmarked even by a church service. Arriving home on the twenty ninth of December, Andrew Cargill tells Henri that there's to be a grand party at his father in law's house and he's to deliver the Frenchman there.

They left France reeling at the news that the King has written to Frederick William II of Prussia asking him, and his fellow European monarchs to help him regain his authority. There's been anger in the Assembly at the news. It has forced Louis to give public assent to the Civil Constitution of the Clergy.

Thirty-nine of the deputies who are also clergymen take the oath of allegiance to the nation. However, they are in the minority and there are tensions in the meetings. Jacob's work is even harder, and there will be little rest for him over the holidays.

They stopped along the way to collect the items Jessamine wanted for herself and the girls, and a set of nine pins for young Stephen. No doubt he'll be playing with the game while the family are gathered in the ballroom of the country house.

Below deck in the ship, there's a new crew member. Etienne was seasick for his first few days at sea, but he's shaping up just fine at his duties. He's going home to his mother, if only as a sailor, visiting the islands. Jacob got another lawyer to countersign the articles of freedom for Etienne and his mother. Below the signatures of Henri Deschamps are those of Jacob Rose and Georges Danton. In a few days, the signature of Jessamine's father will complete the deed. The lad and his mother will have no claim to Half Moon, but they will be free. Cargill has insisted similar papers are signed for all of Claud Deschamps' island families.

The words of the Declaration of Arbroath come to mind: freedom, which no honest man gives up but with life itself.

Jessamine and the girls are waiting for him at the door, but Stephen runs to greet his father and the Frenchman. When they go inside, into the firelit hallway, and the door closes, it begins to snow.

Author's Note

I began the Scottish Agent series with the explosive events of 1789 in mind, and introduced the Rose family- Jacob, Jean the clerk and Jacques the agent provocateur. The seed of the novel was the real-life JA Rose- a man so self-effacing that we only know his initials and not his full name. I can only find two references – one in Kith and Kin, a clan history guide describes him as the inspiration for the Scarlet Pimpernel; the other Electric Scotland names him as the Usher to the Assembly who arrested Robespierre. He was appointed as executor to Mirabeau and responsible for hiding people away from the Guillotine once the Terror began. History has its rock stars- Wellington, Nelson, Napoleon and Robespierre are just a few examples, but it is also populated by ordinary people who do extraordinary things. Electric Scotland introduced me to another Rose- George Rose from Brechin, who rose to prominence under William Pitt the Younger and was a close friend of Lord Nelson. The Rose clan were among the survivors of the Jacobite rebellions- they made a point of courting both sides and saved their fortunes. I took a calculated guess that these two men could have maintained some correspondence throughout one of the more turbulent periods of history.

During the writing of the Scottish Agent novels, I rely heavily on online resources. They tell me that while there was a Morgue in Paris from 1790 onwards, with records available from 1798, I cannot find earlier references, so I have taken the liberty of having the building under construction and staffed by three characters from history. We know Marie Grosholz much better as Madame Tussaud.

Julie MP Adams

Pentemont Abbey, like the convent at Longchamps, which appears in the 1789 novel, gave accommodation to unmarried women and to those seeking shelter when a marriage failed. Residents included the future Empress Josephine, Marie Joseph Rose Beauharnais, whose first marriage was unhappy, and she lived there with her children and a servant, Marie Lannoy who was with her for most of her life. The abbey hosted some salons which were home to political discourse. Manon Roland and Olympe des Gouges were two of the women who played an important part in seeking political change. Des Gouges, along with writers including de Saint Mery, Raynal and Viefville des Essars, was a fervent campaigner for the abolition of slavery.

The events of 1790 might seem less explosive than the previous year, but they include some very significant changes, including the removal of property from the Church and a challenge to the Pope; mutiny among the armed forces and the end of feudal courts. The changes to the economy saw the exile of Necker, without whom the Revolution might never have happened. They also signalled the start of rebellions in the Caribbean against slavery and colonial rule.

The main purpose of this series is to look at the key events of the French Revolution from the point of view of people who are not the most important but are living through those years. In 1789, I included a crime story- the abduction of Lucette. Lucette appears also in this volume and her story will continue through the series. In Women of the Revolution, the page, Etienne, an enslaved boy of mixed race is a focus for the struggle to end slavery in the French colonies.

The character of Suzanne Gregoire, my villain from 1789 is rather down on her luck in this novel, forced into living on her wits along with the adventuress, Jeanne de la Motte. The button shop where they seek sanctuary in Gutter Lane was a real business which supplied silver goods to tailors in Britain and across Europe. I suspect we are going to meet both ladies in the next volume. Meanwhile we have Virginie Deschamps: manipulative and murderous.

Acknowledgements

As always, huge thanks go to Heather Osborne who works the magic that turns a manuscript into a book.

The 18th C was a time of great change in so many ways, including architecture, and lifestyle. I found the volunteers at National Trust for Scotland in Edinburgh to be wonderfully helpful when I visited the Georgian House in Charlotte Square and Gladstone's Land on the Royal Mile, where the cover illustration was taken. World Virtual Tours Paris guide Patrick showed me round the older parts of Paris, without my needing to get on a plane.

I'm indebted to Vaila who steered me away from using French expressions in the text, which was a weakness in 1789 and one I hope I have corrected.

I owe a huge debt of thanks to the Scriptorium at Arbroath Abbey, in which I spent two mornings over the summer of 2023 as a writer in residence. The chapters that are set in the Abbey took shape during those days, and along with the walking lectures on the industrial past of the town, held during the Arbroath 2020 + 1 Festival, gave me a better understanding of the complexities of the Industrial Revolution and its impact on Scotland's East Coast. During the 18th C the Abbot's House was the site of a thread factory, producing yarn for the mills in the town.

This book is dedicated to my History teacher, the late Sinclair Swanson of Keiss, who instilled a love of historical anecdote that I have carried with me throughout my life.

My writing journey is a lifelong one, but the process of having real books in print began with a suggestion that I do an apprenticeship in writing, which in turn led me to workshops and the course: The Business of Being An Author, offered by Dawn Geddes through Dundee Lifelong Learning.

Thanks to my extended family and my friends who offer support and company throughout the research and writing process and beyond. You know who you are and this volume is winging its way, with some chocolate in time for Christmas.

About the Author

Born, raised and educated on the east coast of Scotland, Julie Adams loves books, book festivals, theatre, live music and long walks on nearby beaches and nature trails.

The first Covid lockdown of 2020 coincided with the end of a long career in education. She finally started an apprenticeship as a novelist, and this is her sixth novel. She publishes poetry and short stories on her blog: joolscaithness.novel.wordpress.com

Printed in Great Britain
by Amazon